SPECIAL MESSAGE TO READERS

This book is published by
THE ULVERSCROFT FOUNDATION,
a registered charity in the U.K., No. 264873

The Foundation was established in 1974 to provide funds to help towards research, diagnosis and treatment of eye diseases. Below are a few examples of contributions made by THE ULVERSCROFT FOUNDATION:

- ★ A new Children's Assessment Unit at Moorfield's Hospital, London.
- ★ Twin operating theatres at the Western Ophthalmic Hospital, London.
- ★ The Frederick Thorpe Ulverscroft Chair of Ophthalmology at the University of Leicester.
- ★ Eye Laser equipment to various eye hospitals.

If you would like to help further the work of the Foundation by making a donation or leaving a legacy, every contribution, no matter how small, is received with gratitude. Please write for details to:

**THE ULVERSCROFT FOUNDATION,
The Green, Bradgate Road, Anstey,
Leicestershire, LE7 7FU. England.
Telephone: (0533) 364325**

THE TALKING CLOCK

Jailed for vagrancy in Minnesota, Johnny and Sam woke up to find that one of their cell mates had been murdered during the night. Facing a murder charge they broke jail and set out to find the killer in a wild tangle of suspects, but always the trail led back to the fabulous Talking Clock. The dead man's millionaire grandfather owned the priceless timepiece, and though a lot of people wanted to take it away from him, only one—which one?—had killed to get it.

*Books by Frank Gruber
in the Linford Mystery Library:*

THE HONEST DEALER
THE ETRUSCAN BULL
THE TALKING CLOCK

FRANK GRUBER

THE TALKING CLOCK

Complete and Unabridged

LINFORD
Leicester

First Linford Edition
published March 1990

Copyright © 1940, 1941 by Frank Gruber
All rights reserved

British Library CIP Data

Gruber, Frank
 The talking clock.—Large print ed.—
 Linford mystery library
 I. Title
 823'.914

ISBN 0-7089-6846-5

Published by
F. A. Thorpe (Publishing) Ltd.
Anstey, Leicestershire

Set by Rowland Phototypesetting Ltd.
Bury St. Edmunds, Suffolk
Printed and bound in Great Britain by
T. J. Press (Padstow) Ltd., Padstow, Cornwall

1

OLD Simon Quisenberry was going to die. He was only four years past his allotted three score and ten, but he'd put too much strain on the old heart and two years ago, Dr. Wykagl had given him only six months more. He'd made a liar of the doctor by eighteen months.

It wouldn't be nineteen months. Old Simon knew that and he sat in his wheel chair and listened to the ticking of the clocks as they tolled the moments that were left him. There were a thousand clocks and each told the same story. Each tick a second, sixty ticks a minute, a thousand ticks a thousand seconds. . . . No, a thousand ticks were only one second.

Simon scowled at the clocks. They were confusing him. Damn the things. He'd put so much into them and now at the end, they were betraying him. They were ticking out his life—too fast.

There were a thousand clocks. They were of all shapes and sizes. Some were new, some old. Simon had gathered them from the corners of the earth, had delved into history to acquire some. A fifteenth century papal prince had owned one, another had been the prized possession of a Russian czar. The mistress of an archbishop had owned another and an eighteenth century pirate had gone to the gallows wearing one.

The clocks ticked, the grandfather clock in the corner, the tiny jeweled piece in the glass case, the burnished brass table model, from which a rooster crowed the hour, twenty-four times a day.

All the clocks ticked. All reminded Simon of the brief time he had left. His old blue eyes glared fiercely at the clocks and he dropped his withered hand on the bell that stood on the table beside his chair.

A servant came quietly into the room. Simon couldn't remember his name.

There had been so many servants, since Bonita had taken over the management of the house. They came and went so fast that Simon couldn't even remember their faces. He scowled at the one he saw now.

"Stop the clocks," he ordered.

The servant looked around the room. "You mean . . . all of them?"

"Of course, you fool!" Simon snapped. "I don't want to hear another tick out of any of them. Stop them all."

It was a herculean task that Simon ordered. The man had been employed to keep the clocks running. He wound those that needed winding, pulled the weights of those that operated by weights. He had been taught to keep the clocks running, but not to stop them.

Before he had clumsily stopped the third clock, Simon Quisenberry, purple from anger, wheeled himself out of the room. He summoned another servant.

"I want you to telephone the factory," he instructed. "Tell my son to come out here and bring Nicholas Bos with him. Let me know when they arrive."

Simon Quisenberry looked about the small circle of those interested in his affairs and was not pleased with what he saw.

He said to his son, Eric, "Maybe it's my fault that you're what you are, but if you'd had the stuff you'd have pinned my ears down—and I'd have liked it."

Eric was forty-nine. He was well-built and wore tweeds when he wasn't wearing riding breeches, boots and a broad-brimmed Stetson hat. Eric looked all heman. He only looked it. He flushed under his father's sarcasm and shot an apprehensive glance at his wife, Bonita, who was regarding him with open contempt.

He said: "You're not being fair, Father. You put me into the business and you never let me have any authority."

"Of course I didn't," snapped Simon. "If you'd been man enough you'd have taken the authority. Well, I've got a surprise for you, Eric. I'm leaving you the business. It's yours, all yours. All you've got to do is pay off one million dollars of indebtedness."

Eric Quisenberry blinked. "A million . . ."

"One million dollars. That's what the Quisenberry Clock Company owes the bank. You've got six months. If you can convince the bank, at the end of that time, that there's a chance of paying them the million, they'll give you the chance. If they don't think so—they'll take over and you'll be reading the want ads, which might be a very good thing for you. . . . Were you going to say something, Bonita?"

Bonita Quisenberry was Eric's second wife. She admitted to thirty-five, looked forty and was actually forty-five. She was tawny and beautiful, if you like tigresses. She was about as subtle as a buzz saw. She said to her father-in-law, "I was going to ask you about the clocks. You know I've always been fascinated by them and I thought—"

Simon grunted. "Yes, you've thought. You've thought: 'They're driving me crazy. If it wasn't for the senile old fool's money I'd break every clock in the house.' Isn't that what you've thought, Bonita? You don't have to answer. Because you're not getting the clocks. My Greek friend, over there, gets them. Tell them why, Nick."

Nicholas Bos was tall, thin and olive-skinned. He bowed. "Because I am only man appreciate the clock. I am collector of clock, myself. And—" he coughed, politely—"and I am already holding the mortgage on the clock. Is not so, my friend?"

"Yep," agreed Simon Quisenberry. "One time when I was hard-pressed Nick plunked down a half million dollars, in return for which I gave him a mortgage on every clock in the house but one, he to foreclose said mortgage on the event of my death . . ."

"But that one clock, Mr. Quisenberry," murmured the Greek. "She is most valuable clock of all. I will giving you fifty thousand dollar for her."

"At which price it would be cheap, Nicholas. Still, it's no sale. The Talking Clock I leave to my grandson, Tom Quisenberry, who—" the old man's voice rasped in his throat—"who may develop into as big a thief and scoundrel as his grandfather. He has already shown striking evidence of that by stealing the Talking Clock."

Simon looked fiercely from one to the other of those gathered about him. His eyes came to rest on Eric, his son. "All right, he stole the clock. But he had nerve enough to do it. And he had nerve enough to tell you, his father, to go jump in the Hudson River. The boy's entitled to the clock. I only hope he knows how much it's worth, because it's the most valuable thing I'm leaving." His nostril's flared. "Still hoping, Eric? Well, don't. The business is yours, for six months. This place is yours, for less than six months, since the bank will be pressing you soon.

Yep, it's mortgaged to the last nickel. . . . Did you say something, Bonita?"

The natural color had receded from Bonita Quisenberry's face so that the rouge showed up like irregular red islands. Her nostrils flared and her eyes flashed. She said: "Damn you, you old buzzard!"

Simon laughed. It was a cackling, brittle laugh. "I would have been disappointed if you had held that in, Bonita."

2

BONITA QUISENBERRY was the first to leave the house. She stood for a moment on the broad veranda, regarding the grounds with distaste. She had never liked Twelve O'Clock House from the moment she had come to it, four years ago.

The house itself was sumptuous enough for Bonita's tastes; but Simon Quisenberry was mad on the subject of clocks. It wasn't bad enough that he had the entire house full of crazy clocks, he had to extend the clock motif to the house and grounds.

The house was built on the summit of a steep hill and with it, as a hub, twelve macadamized paths fell away, with the symmetrical precision of a clock dial. The strip that indicated six o'clock was the automobile drive down to the main gate.

Bonita Quisenberry walked down this drive, a distance of a hundred yards. There was a stone cottage beside the gate and as she approached it, a swarthy, heavy-set man came out. He looked beyond Bonita toward the house, then said:

"What's up Bonita? You look like a cat whose mouse has been taken away."

Bonita gave the man a cool look, then entered the cottage. The man followed her in and closed the door.

"Aren't you taking a chance?" he asked. "I let Eric in a little while ago."

"I know and I don't give a damn," Bonita retorted. "I don't give a damn about anything. I'm about ready to call it quits. The old man played me a last, dirty trick."

Joe Cornish, who was nominally the estate manager, looked inquiringly at Bonita. "He's only got a matter of days, hasn't he? And then comes the cake."

"That's the dirty trick. There won't be any cake. He just told us. He's mortgaged everything there is. The sheriff's only holding off until he croaks." Bonita's face twisted angrily. "Can you beat it? I marry that panty-waist, Eric, because he's got a millionaire father who already has one foot in the grave and the other on a fresh banana peel. And what happens? The old man's hocked everything he owns and ever owned and there won't be a dime when he kicks the gong. So I've wasted the best four years of my life."

Joe Cornish's dark brown eyes glittered. "They haven't been exactly wasted have they, Bonita?" He slipped a muscular arm about her waist, and drawing her close, kissed her on her scarlet mouth. He released her after a moment and said, "Besides, there'll be a *few* dollars you can glom onto."

"Joe," said Bonita, looking sullenly at the swarthy estate manager, "sometimes I think I could kill you."

He laughed. "I'll bet you could, at that."

Angrily, she moved to the door. As she opened it, she saw Eric Quisenberry coming down the drive.

He had seen her, so she stood her ground. When he came up, he said, "Am I interrupting something?"

"You're not," she retorted. Then as he continued toward the gate, "You want me to come along and break the news to her? Or don't you think I know about the angelic Ellen?"

He did not answer. When he reached the gate, he went through without looking back.

He walked stiffly down the hill through the village of Hillcrest to the modest apartment house where Ellen Rusk lived. She was at home and greeted him with her usual calm reserve.

"Hello, Eric."

Ellen Rusk was forty-five, but her skin was as smooth as it had been twenty years ago. It did not have the tautness of Bonita Quisenberry's.

Eric took a quick turn about the living room, then faced Ellen Rusk and said, bitterly, "I'm through. Dad is cutting me off without a cent. He's mortgaged and borrowed on everything he ever owned.

Even the company. I'd always thought he'd leave me that, at least. But he isn't. After six months I'll be up on the beach. It's pretty late to start all over."

A frown creased Ellen Rusk's forehead. She said, quietly, "Things will work out somehow, Eric."

"How? I've never had a chance. He treated me like a child—or an imbecile—and now he throws it up to me." He laughed shortly. "Well, it'll solve one problem, anyway. Bonita."

Ellen said, quickly, "No, Eric, you shouldn't—"

"I shouldn't. But she will. She married me for my money and then found I didn't have any. Now, she won't stick it out a day. . . . You were the one I should have married, Ellen."

Ellen Rusk's head came up. She smiled, a half-sad smile. "It's rather late for that, Eric."

"I know," he groaned. "I should have broken with him twenty-five years ago. Perhaps things would have been different. But Ellen, *is* it too late?"

"Yes," she whispered. "There's Diana . . . and Tom . . ."

The mention of his son's name caused Eric to wince. "Father's the fondest of Tom of anyone. And Tom . . . stole the Talking Clock that he's always guarded like the crown jewels."

Ellen inhaled sharply. "Eric, you don't know that Tom did that—"

"Oh, but I do. The clock disappeared when Tom went off. Up to now, Dad never said anything about it. But he admitted today that Tom stole the clock . . . and Tom probably sold it for a fraction of what it's worth and squandered the money."

"You've never heard from Tom?"

He shook his head. "Not even a postcard. I—I've been thinking of him. Hasn't Diana heard from him?"

"No. She's been worried, too. I do believe they were—Shh! that's Diana now."

It was. She came into the apartment. Carrying her latch key. She was a tall slender girl of about twenty. A lean, dark-complexioned man in his early thirties was with her. His eyes widened in surprise when he saw Eric Quisenberry, but the surprise changed to an expression of satisfaction.

"Hello, Mr. Quisenberry. I've been looking all over for you. Hoped I'd—"

Eric regarded the man with considerable distaste. "I only left the office two hours ago—"

"It's Tom!" cut in Diana Rusk. "He's in trouble."

"Perhaps I'd better explain," Wilbur Tamarack said. "They telephoned the office right after you left. Rather than relay the message by phone, I thought I'd run out to Hillcrest. You see, the call was a long-distance one. It came from some sheriff somewhere in Minnesota. They're holding Tom."

"Why?"

Tamarack winced. "I'm afraid it's—"

"Burglary!" cried Diana. "But that's ridiculous. Tom wouldn't do anything like that. I know. We've got to help him."

Eric Quisenberry looked from Diana Rusk to her mother. "How can we help him, if he's in Minnesota? How'd he get away out there in the first place?"

"What difference does it make how he got there?" Diana exclaimed. "We've got to help him, no matter where he is. We —I mean, I'm going out to where he is."

Eric Quisenberry blinked. "You, Diana? Why would you want to go all the way out there? That's my job, Diana . . . I guess."

When Eric returned to Twelve O'Clock House, Bonita was waiting for him on the veranda. "Did Wilbur Tamarack find you?" she asked, then answered the question herself. "Yes, I can see from your face. So your son's in jail? For burglary. What do you think of him, now?"

Eric clenched his hands, hanging at his sides. "The same as I always did. He's my son. I forgot that for a while, when you worked on me. I'm going to him."

"Now?" cried Bonita. "With your father going to die any minute?"

Eric gave her a contemptuous glance and entered the house. He went straight to his father's room. The old man was still in his wheel chair and for an instant before he raised his head, Eric got a glimpse of the real Simon Quisenberry, a frightened old man who had lived too much and now felt the thread slipping through his fingers.

Then Simon saw him and bristled. "What do you want? Think I'm going to change my mind?"

"It's Tom, Father," said Eric Quisenberry. "I've just received word. He's in trouble."

The fierce old eyes glared. "What sort of trouble? Where is he?"

"In Minnesota, a town called Brooklands. They've arrested him. It's pretty serious. Burglary."

"Burglary!" snorted the old man. "That's nonsense. Tom wouldn't commit burglary. He wouldn't steal from strangers." Simon's face twisted. "What are you waiting here for? Why aren't you on your way to him?"

Eric's forehead creased. "But you, Father? . . ."

"What about me? I'm all right. I know I'm going to shove off, but I've made my peace—the way I see it—and there's nothing else to do. But you've got to get Tom out of his jam. Now, get going to him, or by God, I'll have you thrown out of this house—tonight!"

3

THE old one about making a loud noise outside the door on Christmas Eve and then coming in and telling the small boy that Santa Claus has just been shot, had been retired in Johnny Fletcher's youth, but now Johnny Fletcher knew how that small boy had felt.

He stared at the express agent for five full seconds before he could gasp:

"What did you say?"

"I said, the express charges are nine dollars and forty-two cents."

Beside Johnny Fletcher, burly Sam Cragg reeled and cried out in agony. "He sent them *collect?*"

"I don't know about *them,*" the express agent said, laconically, "but there's nine forty-two charges on that there case."

A violent shudder ran through Johnny

Fletcher's lean frame. Then he said, desperately, "Look, Mister, I'm only a book salesman. I've had a little hard luck. My car collapsed in Bemidji. My assistant and I walked from there to here, because we knew these books would be here waiting for us. We're broke, flat broke. We haven't got a dime between us, but in that box are enough books to get us back on our feet. Now, if you could trust us until tomorrow I could sell enough books in that time to pay the charges—"

"No," said the agent. "The express company doesn't do business that way. If you can't pay the charges, the stuff'll have to go back to the shipper."

"Suppose the sender can't pay the charges either, what then?"

"Then we sell the box for the express charges."

"But that's ridiculous! Why, you'd have to hold it a full year before you could sell it and then, you'd get only your express charges out of it—if you're lucky enough to find a buyer. Look, I'll make you a proposition. That box contains a hundred books that I'll sell for $2.95 each. Let me open the box, take out only four books. . . . I'll sell them inside of a half hour—even in a dull burg like this—then I'll come back and pay you the full charges. That's a sporting proposition, isn't it?"

The express agent said, coldly, "Nine forty-two, or no books. That's the only proposition that the express company will make."

"Then keep the books!" roared Sam Cragg. "Keep them and—" He told the express agent what to do with them.

The agent smiled thinly. "You boys are really flat broke? You haven't got even a dollar?"

"Of course we haven't," snarled Johnny Fletcher. "Would we be here so early in the morning, before breakfast, if we had any money?"

"No," said the agent, nodding. "I didn't think so. Well, it so happens that in addition to being the express agent, I'm also the town constable and we've got a village ordinance against vagrants. So, I'll

21

just have to take you boys over to the lockup. Come along, quietly, now, or—"

The alternative was never issued, for Johnny Fletcher and Sam Cragg almost took the door from its hinges in their sudden exodus from the express office. When the express agent-constable got to the sidewalk, Johnny and Sam were a half block up the street, just getting into their real stride.

They did not slacken their speed until they were well outside the town limits. Then Johnny Fletcher slowed up sufficiently for Sam Cragg to catch up. Sam wheezed like a New York taxicab.

"That's the dirtiest trick Mort Murray ever played on us. Sending those books express collect! He should have known by our collect telegram that we were broke."

Johnny shook his head. "It almost makes a fellow lose his faith in humanity. I can't understand it. Mort never let us down before. After all, we don't owe him so much. Just a few hundred."

"It's the Hoodoo," cried Sam. "It's been following us ever since we entered this state. Look, we went to the state fair. They get the biggest attendance there of any state fair in the country—as a rule. But what happened this year? It rained every day of the fair and the only people that came out were those who carried their own canoes with them. Then we came up to this Iron Range and our jalopy, which had only 160,000 miles on it, went all to pieces. And now—*this!*"

"This," said Johnny, bitterly, "and in a strange country, with winter coming on. No overcoats, no books, no car. No nothing."

Sam Cragg inhaled sharply. For him to complain was natural, but Johnny Fletcher—he gave his friend a startled glance.

"Oh, it could be worse, Johnny," he said, backtracking. "Shucks, we've been broke lots of times and we always came out okay. You'll think of something, Johnny. You always have."

"Not here," said Johnny, sadly. "I'm licked out in the wilderness. I doubt if I could even rub two boy scouts together and make a fire—if we had anything to cook over a fire."

"Hey!" cried Sam, alarmed. "Don't give up. There must be some towns and cities in this country. . . . Look, there's a road sign, now . . . Brooklands, two miles. That ain't so far."

"With a population of probably two hundred and ninety-four. You can't pull anything in a town of that size. The natives are too suspicious. Why, I'll bet they wouldn't even cash a check for a fellow."

Sam Cragg scowled. "That reminds me, there might be something in this book." He reached to his hip pocket and brought out a paper-bound book that bore the title, *Twenty Simple Card Tricks*.

Johnny sighed. "Put it away, Sam. Card tricks won't help. Now, if it told how to lay the note . . . but that wouldn't be any good either. I haven't got a note to lay."

Johnny was referring to that little pastime in which certain devious gentlemen engaged. This little pastime consisted of going to stores with a ten-dollar bill, making a small purchase and then engaging in confusing exchanges of money, which somehow always resulted in the storekeeper losing money.

Johnny himself had never "laid the note" but he was almost desperate enough to attempt it . . . if he'd had the ten-dollar bill that was necessary to begin.

Brooklands was, as Johnny had gloomily predicted, a metropolis of around three hundred population. It consisted of a short street of store buildings and a few scattered residences on abbreviated side streets.

A ruddy-cheeked man of about fifty watched them approach the first building. When they came abreast of him, he stepped out and blocked their passage.

"Lookin' for somebody, boys?" he asked, pleasantly.

"Who wants to know?" Johnny demanded, truculently.

"Why, I reckon I do, boys. I'm the constable. . . . Whoa! . . ." He reached to his hip and whipped out a horse pistol that had undoubtedly seen service during the Civil War.

Johnny and Sam gave up their contemplated flight. Johnny said: "What's the idea?"

"My cousin from Poplar City telephoned. Said a couple of boys were headed this way." He winked. "We get two bucks apiece for vags. County's got a lot of roadwork. Well, come along, boys."

He waved the light artillery and Johnny and Sam trudged wearily to the jail at the far end of town, a surprisingly well-built one-story building.

A narrow room in front was evidently the constable's office. To one side was a door made of criss-crossed straps of steel. The constable unlocked this door.

"In you go, boys. You got nothin' to do the rest of the day. In the morning, the judge'll give you thirty days. Thirty days to help improve our nice roads. . . . What did you say, Fatty?"

Sam Cragg said, over his shoulder, "I hope your wife puts arsenic in your apple cider."

Then he turned to survey the jail. It wasn't a bad jail, as jails went. The room was large enough for a dozen beds and contained only five; substantial iron beds, complete with mattresses.

There were two inmates already in the jail, a youth of about twenty, who wore a suit of good material, even though it was somewhat spotted and wrinkled, and an old-timer, a regular bindle stiff.

The kid said, "Welcome to our hotel." There wasn't much enthusiasm in his tone.

"Howdy, folks," Johnny said, pleasantly. "My name's Fletcher and this big fellow is Sam Cragg."

The boy smiled wanly. "My name's Tom Quisenberry."

"Glad to know you." Johnny looked at the older hobo. The latter caught his eye, shook his head and mumbled something under his breath. Johnny shrugged and, moving to one of the beds, tested the mattress.

"Not bad," he commented. "Not good, but not bad."

Sam Cragg dropped his two hundred and twenty pounds onto one of the beds. He grunted. "It'll do. I think I'll catch me some rest to get in shape for that roadwork."

Johnny Fletcher winced. "Yeah, the roadwork." He looked at the boy. "The conny said they work the vags on the road. How come you two are taking it easy?"

Tom Quisenberry frowned. "He just came in a couple of hours ago and me—I guess, I'm not classified as a tramp. I'm waiting trial."

"Oh-oh," said Johnny. "Don't tell me, now—you held up the Union Pacific, huh?"

Young Quisenberry chewed at his lower lip. "It's not funny to me. In fact, I feel like hell."

4

GRIPING about it never made any jail more comfortable. When you're in, you're in, and you might as well make the most of it. After a couple of hours of listening to Tom Quisenberry complain, Johnny Fletcher said,

"Why, look, Kid, there are mattresses on these beds. That's something. Down in the Bloomington Illinois jail one time, I slept on a bare spring and you could play tick-tack-toe on my back for a month afterwards."

"Yah," Sam Cragg said "and tell him about the time we was in jail in Pacific, Missouri. You know, that rathole in which they stuck eighteen of us and it was so crowded we had to take turns standing and sitting."

The Kid sat on one of the beds (with mattress). His chin hung almost to his knees. He said, without looking up:

"You fellows are used to it. But this is the first time I've ever been in a jail."

Sam Cragg sang in a bar room bass:

"Sittin' in the jailhouse, back against the wall,
A red he-headed woman was the cause of it all. . . ."

Johnny Fletcher shot a dirty look at Cragg. "No one ever gets used to a jail." He appealed to the hobo, who so far had not spoken a word. "Do they, Old-Timer?"

The only difference between Old-Timer and Pete the Tramp, the cartoon character, was that Old-Timer had a beard and looked a lot worse than Pete. Johnny wouldn't have been surprised to see Old-Timer's clothes get up and walk off without him.

He made no answer to Johnny Fletcher's question. He was past the stage where it was worth answering questions put to him by anyone less than a cop.

Johnny knew that Old-Timer's horrible example, as much as anything else, had thrown Quisenberry into his fit of despondency. But he was determined to do his Boy Scout deed for the day and he kept after the Kid. There wasn't anything else to do in the jail, anyway.

"It's all in the way you look at it. Here we are, four of us, in a little jug somewhere up on the Iron Range, in Minnesota. . . . What *is* the name of this burg, anyway, Sam?"

Sam Cragg shrugged. "Poplar City, maybe. No—that was the other burg."

Johnny Fletcher winced. "Where we discovered that Mort Murray had sent us the books, express collect, and we didn't have the dough to get them out of hock. That wasn't very kind of Mort."

Sam Cragg scowled. "It wasn't very kind of us not to pay Mort when we had the dough. You know Mort's only one jump ahead of the sheriff, usually. *We* couldn't even keep that one jump ahead of him."

"My pal," muttered Johnny. He turned to young Quisenberry. "What're you in for?"

The boy flushed. "I was hungry. I didn't have any place to sleep and there wasn't anyone around and the store window was open. . . ."

"So you climbed in and tapped the till?"

The Kid nodded, his face turning a deep crimson. "The proprietor was sleeping in the back of the store."

Johnny said, "Burglary. That's not so good. They might give you six months—"

"Six months!" cried Sam. "Two to five years more likely. In the state pen too, not any comfy hotel like this. Why—" He looked at Johnny and subsided.

The Kid was about ready to break into tears. Johnny wondered why the hell he had ever left home.

"You—you think they'll give me that much?"

Johnny looked fiercely at Sam Cragg.

"Nah. Sam's kidding. But look, you got a family somewhere."

The boy started to shake his head, then bobbed it up and down suddenly. "Yes, my—my father. I think they've already notified him. That's why—what I'm worrying about. I didn't want him to know. But they found a letter on me. I wouldn't have minded it half so much if only Dad wouldn't know. Or . . ."

"A girl?"

The Kid nodded. "I got kicked out of school and Dad raised a fuss. I told him I'd go it on my own and—well, I couldn't make it. That's all there's to it."

"Why, hell!" exclaimed Johnny. "You haven't got anything to worry about. Your old man'll come here and hire a good lawyer and they'll probably get you off with a suspended sentence. You'll be back in that college of yours while Sam and I are still doing our thirty-day road job. Right, Old-Timer?" He appealed again to the professional tramp.

Old-Timer didn't answer. He sat on his bunk, back against the brick wall, knees drawn up to his chin. His hat was tilted over his face and he seemed asleep.

Sam Cragg took a battered pack of playing cards from his pocket and began shuffling them. Johnny groaned. His friend's hands were better suited to breaking rocks than manipulating a deck of cards.

"Take a card, Kid," Sam said, brightly, extending the fanned deck.

The boy shook his head. "I don't feel like it."

Undiscouraged, Sam held the deck out to Johnny. The latter took a card and looked at it. "All right, what do I do now?"

Sam held out half of the deck. "Lay it on there." Johnny obeyed and Sam put the other half of the deck on top and began fumbling with the cards. One fell to the floor.

Johnny said, "Yeah, that's the card."

Sam reddened. "That wasn't the trick. I was going to put the whole pack in a handkerchief and then show you how I could force your card right through the cloth."

"Better read your book some more," Johnny said, sarcastically.

Muttering to himself, Sam took from his pocket the book: *Twenty Simple Card Tricks*.

Johnny yawned. "Me, I'm going to sleep. Tell the porter to wake me when we get to the end of the line."

He stretched out on his bunk and fell promptly asleep.

He woke hours later. Tom Quisenberry was beside his bunk, whispering. "Mr. Fletcher," he said, "don't say anything. Just take this, will you? Give it back to me in the morning. . . ." He thrust a card into Johnny's hand and padded back to his own bunk.

Johnny waited a minute, then turned over. The Kid had settled back on his own bed. Sam Cragg's burly form was outlined just beyond. Johnny rolled back to the other side. Yes, Old-Timer was still on his own bed. Then, why the mystery? Why should the Kid wake him up in the middle of the night, slip him a card and give him the hugh-hush act?

He was still thinking about it, when he fell asleep again. He dreamed that he was riding on a Seventh Avenue subway train and that a pickpocket, disguised as a *Daily Worker* newsboy, was rolling him. He hit the *Daily Worker* lad so hard that Joe Stalin yowled . . . and then he woke up and the town constable was banging on the bars of the door with a tin cup and yelling: "Rise and shine, boys! The judge is going fishing and he wants to get you fellows out of the way early. You bums, come on out and take your medicine."

Johnny yawned at Sam Cragg across the Kid's sleeping form. "When he talks about bums, does he mean us, Sam?"

Sam got up, stretched and said, "Yow! . . ."

He leaned over and shook the Kid. "Hey, Kid, wake up. The porter wants to make up your berth. . . ." Suddenly, Sam exclaimed and bent to peer into the Kid's face. Then his mouth fell open and an expression of horror distorted his face.

"Gawd!" he said.

Johnny Fletcher took one glance at his friend's face, then stopped over the boy on the bed and shock rippled through him.

The boy was lying on his side, eyes glassy and bulging. Livid, red welts were on the throat. He had evidently been strangled.

By this time the constable saw that something was wrong. "What's—what's the matter with him?"

Johnny turned. "He's . . . dead."

"Dead? Why . . . why . . ." The constable's eyes fluttered wildly, then he turned the big key in the lock and pulled the door open. He started to come into the cell but didn't, for what happened was so sudden and unexpected that even Johnny Fletcher, alert as he usually was, was caught flatfooted.

Old-Timer, the tramp, came up from his bunk and made a rush for the door. A knife flashed in his hand and he struck at the constable. Johnny saw the expression on the constable's face, heard his cry of pain, and catapulted through the door after the tramp.

Old-Timer was bolting through the street door, and in passing reached out a hand and slammed the door in Johnny's face. By the time Johnny got it open and hit the street, Old-Timer had a fifty-foot start on him.

It suddenly dawned on Johnny then, that there was something terribly wrong about Old-Timer. He was running as no man of his years or appearance had ever run before. He was gaining on Johnny, on a straightaway track.

Behind Johnny, Sam Cragg yelled hoarsely. "Johnny! Wait for me."

A couple of the village shopkeepers, letting down awnings in preparation for a hot sun, turned from their work to watch the three men dashing down the main street of the town. But when they saw the constable stagger out of the jail, clutching his side, and heard him crying out: "Stop them! They murdered me," they ran into their stores.

A hundred feet ahead of Johnny, the

tramp whipped around a corner and when Johnny turned it, Old-Timer was in a battered flivver already shooting away.

Johnny groaned and stopped. He stared after the disappearing flivver until Sam caught up to him.

"We gotta keep going, Johnny," Sam panted. "That goddam tramp stabbed the constable—and did for the Kid."

"I know," said Johnny. "And did you see him run? No sixty-year-old bum ever ran like that. Say . . ." He thrust a hand into his pocket and brought out the card the Kid had forced on him during the night.

He looked at it and whistled, softly. "A pawn ticket. 'Uncle Joe, The Friend In Need. Columbus, Ohio'. . . . I don't get it."

Sam Cragg exclaimed nervously. "If we hang around, they'll get us. For breaking jail, if not murder . . ."

"Right you are, Sam," Johnny said. "We've got to put miles behind us. Something tells me that that bum isn't going to be easy to catch and the boys here'll pin the Kid's murder on whoever they can grab—namely Samuel Cragg and John Fletcher. Let's travel...."

5

THEY traveled. Reaching the edge of the little town, they cut across an open field to a patch of woods and stalked through it as silently as the Indians of old—after said Indians had imbibed too freely of the white man's firewater.

Neither was much on the pioneer stuff. Burly Sam Cragg, in as fine physical condition as a man can be, was the first to complain of the rough going. "My feet are killing me, Johnny. Can't we take a rest?"

Johnny Fletcher peered back at the solid wall of poplars. "We haven't come more than a couple of three miles, Sam. They'll be after us by now. Maybe with bloodhounds."

"Bloodhounds!" Sam Cragg's eyes popped open. "Those long-eared mutts they show in the movies? You . . . you suppose they've got some like that up in this goddam country?"

"I don't know," Johnny replied, his forehead creased. "But I do think we ought to put some more miles between us and that burg. They'll shut off the roads and beat the woods. Murder's murder, Sam, even up here in Minnesota."

"But we didn't do it. The bum did. He *must* have. When they catch him..."

"When they catch him, Sam. Stop to think a minute—what did he look like?"

"Why, just a bum. An old guy..."

"Old? Did you see him run? No old guy ever ran like that."

Sam was startled. "Huh? You think maybe he wasn't as old as he looked?"

"Just what did he look like?"

Sam blinked. "Why, like a bum. Maybe fifty-sixty, dirty clothes and a beard...."

"Suppose the beard's a phony? And the clothes a disguise. That car he made the getaway in . . . how'd he know it would be around the corner, with the key in it?"

"You think he had it planted there?

That he knew he was going to make a getaway?"

Johnny shook his head. "I don't know what to think, Sam. Honest, I don't. But doesn't it strike you as screwy? The whole thing. Why would he want to kill the Kid? And then stab the constable?"

"We don't know the Kid was killed. He was dead, yeah. But mightn't he have died naturally?"

Johnny was thoughtful for a moment. Then he took out the pawn ticket. "The Kid woke me up in the middle of the night to give me this. He was scared. Plenty scared. Uh-uh, I say he was murdered. And in view of Old-Timer's actions later . . ."

Sam Cragg got to his feet. "I guess I can go another mile."

"You'll go more than that, Sammy old boy."

They continued through the poplars a half mile and came to a small stream. There Sam had his bright idea. "Say, don't they always walk through water to lose their trail?"

Johnny grinned a twisted grin. "That picture, 'Fugitive From A Chain Gang,' must have made an impression on you. All right, we'll give it a whack. But I'm taking off my shoes...."

Sam Cragg followed Johnny's example, and carrying their shoes and socks, the two began wading upstream. Fortunately, for them, the creek had a gravel bottom and they were able to travel it without too much difficulty. The trouble came with occasional large stones on which they stepped.

They waded for a quarter mile or so, which Johnny Fletcher thought was enough to foil bloodhounds. They dried their feet then, with handkerchiefs, as best they could and put on their socks and shoes. There were holes in the toes of Sam's socks.

The foot bath having refreshed them, Sam made no more complaint. For a mile. Then he thought of his stomach. "Geez, I wish we'd had our breakfast first."

Johnny had already been thinking about that. He had a hunch, however, that it would be some time before they sat down to another square meal. He wondered if hunger would not drive them back into the arms of the law. This country up here was pretty sparsely settled. They had traveled at least four miles from the town where they had been incarcerated and he had yet to see a house.

They sat down on a log to rest a while and then Sam sniffed the air. "I smell smoke. Must be a house around somewheres. Maybe we can get a handout."

Johnny wondered about that. It was at least an hour and a half since their escape. How quickly did news travel in this country?

He got up and looked in the direction he judged to be south. The trees seemed thinner and he thought there was a clearing just beyond.

"C'mon, Sam," he said, "let's see if there's fire by that smoke."

A hundred feet and they saw the clearing, a two- or three-acre patch, in the middle of which stood a ramshackle log cabin. Smoke was coming out of the chimney.

Sam Cragg drew a deep breath. "I haven't done this for a good many years, but here goes. . . ."

He stepped out into the clearing and leaped back instantly as a huge German shepherd dog came out of the cabin and began barking furiously. A man in overalls appeared in the doorway of the house.

"Git him!" he ordered.

The dog was quite willing. He came for the trees with a rush that sent Johnny's heart leaping into his throat. Sam jumped for an overhanging limb, but misjudged the strength of it and it broke with his weight, crashing him to the ground.

Johnny stooped and tore the limb from Sam's hands and whirled just in time to thrust it into the charging dog's face.

"G'wan home, you—" he snarled.

The dog yelped, rushed back a few feet and baring his teeth, set up a furious racket of barking. Sam Cragg scrambled to his feet, found a foot length chunk of decaying wood and threw it at the dog, which dodged it nimbly.

Out in the clearing, the farmer yelled: "Who's there? What are you doing out there?"

"Call off your dog!" Johnny replied, "before he gets hurt!"

Swearing softly, Sam Cragg was breaking off a stout club for himself from another tree limb. "Man's best friend," he muttered.

The farmer came out of the house, gripping a shotgun in his hands. "C'mon out of there, you! . . ." he called.

Johnny groaned. He made a sudden rush for the dog with the tree limb, then wheeled and started for the thicket again. Sam lumbered along behind, turning now and then to threaten the dog which followed.

He was a persistent dog, keeping on their heels long after his master had dropped out of the chase; for almost a mile, in fact.

"That settles the food question," Johnny said, when they had finally lost the canine pursuer. "You won't find a farmhouse up here without a mutt. Besides—I don't think we ought to show ourselves just yet."

"But we've got to eat!" Sam protested.
"Why? People go days and days without food sometimes. Tighten that belt of yours and let's put some more miles behind us. Maybe tomorrow . . ."

Sam Cragg groaned.

It was a warm day and they perspired freely as they ploughed through the woods, crossing dirt roads hurriedly and avoiding clearings and houses. Johnny watched the sun, so that they continued steadily in a more or less southerly direction. Civilization, he judged, was in that direction and he wanted civilization—in big quantities. A city man, he needed a city in which to lose himself.

When the sun was almost overhead, Sam Cragg declared that he could travel no more and threw himself flat on the ground, under a huge cedar tree.

Johnny seated himself beside Sam, resting his back against the tree. The ground looked inviting, but he was afraid if he stretched himself out on it, he would be unable to get up again.

He said: "How about a card trick, Sam?"

Sam's hand moved to his pocket, then fell to his side. "No," he groaned. "Not now."

Johnny grinned wryly as he looked down at his friend. The big fellow's feet were all out of proportion to his massive body. Sam could stand almost any kind of punishment—except walking. Well, Johnny didn't like walking either.

He thought of the bad luck that had dogged them ever since they had entered the State of Minnesota. Six weeks ago, that had been. It had rained every day at the Minnesota State Fair. They had scarcely broken even on the week, after paying their hotel bill and incidentals. Sam had been moving south, then, but Johnny had wanted to see the northern country, the Iron Range.

Disaster had overtaken them up there.

On top of everything they had been jugged for vagrancy in a one-horse town.

And now murder.

He and Sam were innocent of the charge, of course, but they couldn't prove it, locked up. They had to take to their heels. The question was, could they elude capture?

Johnny didn't know. But he was going to give the thing his damndest.

He said to Sam: "Come on, big boy. We've got to go."

Sam rolled over on his broad back and looked bitterly at Johnny. "Go ahead, Johnny. I'll just wait here for the cops."

Johnny laughed without humor. Then, suddenly, he twisted his head sidewards and a glint of alarm came to his eyes. "Quiet, Sam," he said, in a low tone. "Someone's coming. . . ."

Sam promptly sat up. "I hear them . . . sounds like a wagon."

"A wagon! Say . . . cops wouldn't be using a wagon, not even up here in Minnesota. I think I'll just have a look. . . ."

The rumble of wheels and the clop-clop of a horse's hoofs on earth told him the location of the road. On hands and knees Johnny scuttled towards it.

It was no more than fifty feet away and was merely a winding trail cut through the virgin forest, a real backwoods road.

6

THE wagon was approaching leisurely, drawn by a single horse. The lone occupant of the wagon was a bucolic appearing youngster in his early twenties. On impulse, Johnny stepped out into the road.

The youth saw him and pulled up his horse. "Hello there, neighbor," he said cheerily. "Live around here?"

Johnny nodded. "Up the road a ways. How about a lift?"

"Surest thing, neighbor. Hop on." The youth moved obligingly to one side of the wooden wagon seat. Johnny grinned crookedly. "My brother's with me. Okay for him, too?" Then, without waiting for a reply, he turned and called, "Oh, Sam! Man wants to give us a lift home. Hurry up."

Sam Cragg came cautiously out of the woods. The man on the wagon seat nodded, "Hi, neighbor!"

In the act of climbing into the wagon, Johnny looked in the back of it and saw that it was filled with gleaming aluminum pans.

He exclaimed, "Peddler, eh?"

The driver chuckled. "Direct salesman. We don't like the word peddler—not any more." He clapped the lines on the horse's rump and added, "Giddap!" then reached back of him and brought out one of the aluminum kettles.

"Not bad, eh?"

Johnny took the thing in his hand. "No, not bad, at all. What is it?"

"What's it look like, Mister?"

Johnny was sure his guess would be wrong, so merely shook his head. Sam, however, guessed audibly and the salesman roared until the tears rolled down his cheeks.

When he was able to talk, he sputtered. "It does look something like that, but it ain't. It's—it's a chicken fryer. And—and—aw, hell, reach back in one of the boxes and bring out a bottle—two bottles, one from each box."

Johnny brought them out and looked at the label. The one on the larger bottle read: "Four Star Lemon Extract," and the one on the smaller bottle, "Four Star Vanilla Extract."

"Ah," he said, "the old lemon extract. I haven't seen it in years."

The salesman shook his head. "You're right, Mister, she ain't what she used to be. Not no more. Folks is getting too smart. That's why I'm working the dirt roads. The boys like to stick to the pavements with their cars, but me, I got me old Nellie here and she likes the dirt better than the pavement. And so do I. I don't make as many calls in a day as I would on the concrete, but I do just as well in the long run, I guess."

"What's the deal, Mister?" Sam Cragg asked, coming to life.

"I was just going to get to that, gentlemen," the salesman said. "You see this bottle of lemon extract? It's a full sixteen ounces of the best flavoring you ever tasted. What would you figure it'd cost you in the store? A dollar? Cheap at the price. But you know what? I sell it for ninety-nine cents, *and* with each and every bottle—purely for advertising purposes—I give free, absolutely free, mind you, an eight-ounce bottle of this genuine imported domestic vanilla extract. Now, I'm asking you, gentlemen, is that a bargain or isn't it?"

"Is it?" Johnny asked. "So what about the aluminum pot? Where does that come in?"

The salesman looked discomfited. "I was coming to that. I merely wanted to impress on your minds the real bargain you were going to get in this extract deal and then I was going to bowl you over with the clincher. This genuine nonstain, nonrusting, nonbreakable, nonwearing aluminum chicken fryer, yours with the compliments of the Four Star Extract Company. Yes, sir, gentlemen, the whole works, a sixteen-ounce bottle of lemon extract, an eight-ounce bottle of vanilla extract and this beautiful, magnificent chicken fryer, all for the paltry sum of ninety-nine cents. . . . Think of it, gentlemen, this amazing value for only ninety-nine cents. . . ."

"I am thinking of it," Johnny said.

"It's a sale, then? You'll buy?"

Johnny shrugged. "When we get home . . . maybe. You see, Grandma runs the house. But—we'll put in a word, won't we, Sam?"

Sam scowled. "Yeah, sure. When we get home."

"That's splendid," said the direct salesman. "I'll take you up on that. How far ahead do you live?"

"Oh, up a little ways," Johnny replied.

"A mile; two miles?"

"Little farther than that. I'll point out the place when we get there."

The direct salesman frowned. "Well, are you in a hurry? 'Cause if you aren't, I'd like to stop at that farmhouse up there, you know. Save me coming back."

"Sure, sure," Johnny said, easily. "No use passing up business, just because we're along. Go right ahead and stop. . . ."

Sam's eyes were rolling frantically, but Johnny shot him a look of caution.

The house ahead was a log cabin, with mud plastered into the chinks. John was relieved to see that no telephone wire ran from the road to the house. Nevertheless, when the peddler climbed down from the wagon, he got down with him. He wanted to make sure the man said nothing to the woman, that she could relay along.

He followed leisurely behind the peddler as the man made his way toward the door of the farmhouse.

A faded, tired-looking woman came out of the house as they approached. The peddler immediately went into his act.

"Good afternoon, Madam. My name is Clarence Hackett and I'm representing the Four Star Extract Company. You've heard of our firm, of course. The makers of the finest, imported domestic cooking and flavoring extracts. Used by housewives everywhere. This is it right here, Madam. . . ." He went on with his patter, very much as he'd given it to Johnny and Sam in the wagon. When he finished, the woman's eyes lingered on the shiny, aluminum chicken fryer, but she shook her head. "I'm sorry, Mister, but I ain't got no money."

"But, Madam," Clarence Hackett persisted, "it's only ninety-nine cents. Surely, you have that much . . ."

"No, I ain't, Mister," the woman said, sadly. "We're poor people here. I'd sure like to have that there chicken fryer, but I can't buy it. Not today."

Clarence Hackett began to frown, but Johnny Fletcher said, smoothly: "Madam, I see you have some chickens. Leghorns, too. I'll bet they lay a good many eggs."

"They do, that," the farm woman said, "but eggs are way down, only eighteen cents a dozen."

"That's not very much, is it? Well, they'll undoubtedly go much higher before the winter's up. I'll tell you what, Madam, since you like this chicken fryer *and* the extracts, why don't we make a trade? Mmm . . . six dozen eggs come to approximately one dollar, as nearly as we can make it. Why not give us six dozen eggs and we'll give you this...."

Clarence Hackett began to sputter, but Johnny said, out of the side of his mouth, "I'll fix it up with you, later," and the salesman quieted.

The farm woman snapped eagerly at the bargain and in a few minutes Johnny and Clarence Hackett were stowing away a basket of eggs in the wagon and climbing aboard.

"Okay, Mister," Hackett said. Then, "They're your eggs. I'll take the money...."

Johnny nodded. "Swell, soon's we get home.... You find many folks on the back road who're short of money?"

Hackett scowled. "That's the trouble with this business. Those who want to buy haven't got the money. At least, that's the excuse they give. I'd sell three women out of five if I took eggs and chickens trade, instead of money...."

"Well, why don't you?"

Hackett blinked. "Huh? Why, what would I do with them?"

"Sell them. There's a produce dealer in just about every little crossroads town you come to. Get yourself an egg crate and a chicken coop. Suppose it's a little extra trouble. You're making on the deal, aren't you? These six dozen eggs will bring you a dollar and eight cents from any produce dealer. You'd have gotten only ninety-nine cents in cash, *if* you'd made the sale, which you wouldn't have in this case."

Hackett stared at Johnny. "But chickens? Sometimes they haven't got six dozen eggs, what about chickens? How'd I know when I was making out?"

"Get yourself posted on market prices and carry a scale. If the chicken comes to sixty cents, take two chickens. I'm sure they'd trade with you even, on such a basis. Try it and see...."

"Damned if I don't! Why—I've been lucky to make one sale in ten calls. Taking eggs and chickens, boy, I'll clean up. I'll be in the produce business, yeah —but what's the difference?"

"Then, you'll take these eggs?"

"Sure, why not? I'll even deal with you

—I mean your grandmother, on the same basis. We ought to be getting there soon, now. Your home, I mean."

"Not quite," Johnny said, wryly. "It's still quite a piece down the road. In fact —we may not get there today."

"Huh? Where do you live—Minneapolis?"

"Farther than that."

"New York," snarled Sam Cragg.

The peddler whistled. "Then what're you doing away up here? And—" a frown spread across his face—"why the bunk about living up the road?"

"Because we're hitchhiking," Johnny said. "It's customary to tell a pickup you live up the road a piece. You see, old man, we're in practically the same racket you are. We're salesmen, too."

"No wonder you knew how to handle that woman back there. Say, what's your line?"

"Books. Physical culture. We do a strong-man pitch. Sam here is Young Samson. He breaks belts and chains with his chest and then I sell the suckers books telling them how they can get to be as strong as Young Samson."

"Well, where's your outfit?"

"That," said Johnny, "is why we're hitchhiking. We haven't got an outfit. We've had a streak of bad luck. Our car went to pieces and we ran out of supplies —and dough. We're hitchhiking back to New York, now, to get a new stake."

"You'll never get there in this wagon," declared Hackett. "You'd make a lot better time on the concrete roads. . . ."

"And where are they? To tell you the truth, we're lost."

"I'll show you." Hackett reached under his seat and brought out an automobile road map of the kind given away at gasoline stations. "I'll show you where we are now. . . . Right about there. Moose Lake, that's the next town ahead. Not much of a town. But it's only eight miles to Highway 60, the main drag between Duluth and Minneapolis. You want to make for it."

Johnny put his finger on the map, at a

spot named Brooklands. "How far are we from that town?"

"Brooklands? Mmm, about twenty-six miles. You should have cut north from there to the Hibbing road that's paved, instead of cutting south by the shortest roads. Yeah, it's longer, but you'd of made better time on the pavement."

Sam Cragg took a handkerchief from his pocket. He flipped it out and draped it across his left arm. Then he brought out his pack of cards.

"Look, Mister," he said, "I want to show you a trick . . . take a card."

"Ha!" exclaimed Clarence Hackett. "The old handkerchief trick, eh? Here . . . let *me* show you how it's done."

Sam put the cards back into his pocket. "Never mind," he said, in disgust.

7

"NEW YORK license plates," said Johnny Fletcher, stepping out from the foliage at the side of the road. "It's the same car that was going north a few minutes ago."

"This one had a dame," Sam Cragg said.

"So did the first. All alone. And not bad at all. . . . There it turns. . . ."

Sam headed back for the trees, but Johnny remained on the road. "Let's see what it's all about," he called to Sam.

The car was an olive-green coupe. As it hurtled down upon Johnny the driver blasted the air with the horn and began applying brakes. Johnny stepped to the shoulder of the road and the coupe squealed past and made a quick turn in the road.

It slipped up behind him. "Lift, Mister?" called the girl in the coupe.

Johnny pointed to Sam Cragg and smiled. "There's two of us."

"'S all right," said the girl. "I'm not afraid."

Johnny shrugged. "Okay, lady. We're not either. Come on, Sam...."

He opened the door and slipped in beside the girl. Sam Cragg followed warily. It was a tight fit in the coupe, but if the girl didn't mind, Johnny most certainly didn't. She was pretty young, not more than nineteen or twenty. Blond and with nice, fresh features.

She shifted into second, zoomed into high and sent the coupe hurtling southward. "Cars are few up this way," she said. "I passed you and got to thinking that it was pretty far to the next town."

"It's a lot farther to where we're going."

"How far is that? Minneapolis?"

"New York."

"Why, I'm from New York!"

"I saw the license. Uh . . . headin' there now?"

"Not exactly. I—I have some

business. . . . I mean, I'm visiting up here at a resort. Near . . . Brooklands."

Johnny could feel Sam's body against his shudder. He was silent for a moment. Then he said: "Brooklands is back a ways, isn't it?"

Her face turned for an instant to him. He saw that it was clouded. "Why," she said, hesitantly, "don't . . . you know?"

He shook his head. "No. I've never been there." He added instantly. "Maybe I have at that. Yeah."

The wheel swerved just a little.

Johnny said, gently, "I think you'd better let us out. You're pretty young for this sort of thing."

"What do you mean?"

"I mean the New York license plates, the fact that you passed us going north, came back, passed again and returned. To pick us up . . . for a ride?"

"Johnny," exclaimed Sam in alarm.

Johnny nudged him to be quiet. "You're the Kid's . . . girl?"

She gasped. "Then you *are!* I knew it. I had a hunch, when I saw you popping into the woods the first time I passed you. You're the men who were with Tom . . ."

"Who were in jail with him, when it happened. Well . . . do you think we kill—did it?"

The wheel swerved wildly and her foot loosened its pressure on the accelerator. Johnny said, quickly, "We didn't. But if we had, you shouldn't have . . . picked us up. You're just—"

"Who did it?" she cried, fiercely. "If you two didn't, who did?"

"There was another man in jail. A tramp . . ."

"A tramp? An ordinary . . . tramp? Are you sure?"

Johnny shrugged. "I was at the time. You see, the Kid and this tramp were already in jail when we were tossed in. I didn't pay much attention to the tramp, because that's just what he looked like. An old-time bindle stiff." His nose wrinkled. "But the Kid—well, I could see that he wasn't used to anything like that. We got pretty friendly. He'd mentioned that the authorities had notified his family...."

"That was two days ago. I reached Brooklands this morning ... an hour after you ... an hour after you ran away."

"We've been doing Daniel Boone stuff all day," Johnny said ruefully. "Uh ... what're they saying back there? That me and Sam did it?"

She nodded. "All three of you."

"Three? Um. They think we were all together. And ... the Kid?

Her mouth trembled for a moment, but then she stiffened it. "Choked to death ..."

Johnny put his hand into his coat pocket and fingered the pawn ticket that young Tom Quisenberry had given him. He kept it in his pocket.

He said: "What about his family?"

"His father's on the way to Brooklands. Probably just getting there now, since he went by train, I drove. Thirty hours straight through from New York."

Johnny grunted. "What about his mother?"

"There's a stepmother. She—well, it is mainly because of her that Tom left home. But there's Tom's grandfather, Simon Quisenberry. He thought a lot of Tom."

"Simon Quisenberry? Would he be the big clock and watch man?"

"Yes. He owns the Quisenberry Clock Company. He . . . he collects antique clocks, too. He's pretty old—and sick. As a matter of fact, he's not expected to live more than a few days more."

They were approaching a small town, a tiny hamlet really, for it did not contain more than forty or fifty buildings. The girl slowed up going through and Johnny saw the state trooper standing beside his motorcycle at a filling station.

He frowned and looked in the rear-vision mirror. The trooper was rolling his bike out to the concrete slab. He said to the girl:

"Step on it. That cop's coming."

Sam groaned. "Here we go!"

They were slammed back against the leather upholstery, as the girl gave the coupe the gas. Johnny saw the speedometer needle leap from forty-five to fifty-five then to sixty and beyond.

"He's coming," he said. "Slow up when you take the curve ahead and we'll hop out."

"But you can't! . . ." the girl cried desperately.

"Got to," said Johnny grimly. "We can't afford to be taken back. Slow down!"

The car zoomed around the curve and the brakes began squealing as the girl applied them. Sam had the door open before the car came to a halt.

Johnny crowded him. "I've got something of the Kid's!" he cried. "Meet us in Columbus, Ohio. . . ."

Sam leaped to the road shoulder, missed his footing and plunged into a ditch. Johhny jumped, ran headlong to the fringe of brush near-by. In the distance he heard the put-put-put of a roaring motorcycle.

The girl was meshing gears, zooming her car away.

"Duck, Sam!" cried Johnny.

The motorcycle came around the turn as they gained shelter.

Then it was run again. The motorcycle would overtake the girl and she'd tell the trooper that she had picked up a couple of hitchhikers, but that they had dropped off. The cop would come back, search for them a while, then scoot back to the hamlet and turn in the alarm.

In a little while they would be beating the woods here.

Johnny figured out the time element and thought that he had a half hour before the search would become really intensive. When they reached the graveled parallel secondary road a half mile back of the concrete pavement, he went into a trot that had Sam Cragg panting and groaning before they had covered a quarter mile. Then Johnny's perseverance was rewarded. An old, battered flivver of the vintage 1928 was standing in the front yard of a ramshackle frame house.

Johnny went boldly up to it, climbed in and started the motor. He backed the car out to the road where Sam was waiting as a man came running out of the house waving and yelling. Clamping his jaw grimly, Johnny turned the car in the road.

"Come on, Sam!" he ordered.

Sam piled in, complaining. "Car stealing, now!"

"Better than a murder charge, Sam!"

He roared the car up the graveled road at the terrific speed of thirty-two miles an hour. Two miles ahead, he turned right, went three miles, then turned right again.

"Hey, you're going back north!" Sam cried.

"I know. That's one direction they won't expect us to go. If the gas will only hold out. . . . Damn, it shows empty."

He stopped the car and investigated the tank. There were two or three gallons in it. They did not register because the indicator was broken.

Relieved, Johnny started out again.

Stopping again, after a few miles, he consulted his road map acquired from Clarence Hackett, the lemon extract man. He located their position, then turned due east.

Twenty minutes later, still rolling along a secondary graveled road, he said, "Well, here we go into Wisconsin. The cops here shouldn't be fussy about us, since we haven't done anything in their state."

He didn't know that by crossing a state line in a stolen automobile he had violated a Federal statute. It was just as well that he didn't know it, for after a few minutes the motor of the flivver coughed and spit and then expired. The gas tank was bone dry.

They pushed the car to the side of the road. "Here we go, again," Johnny said.

"It'll be dark in a few minutes," Sam said, suggestively.

"Yes? Well, as nearly as I can figure, we're ten to fifteen miles from Spooner, Wisconsin."

"Never heard of it."

"That shows your ignorance, Sam. Spooner, Wisconsin happens to be a railroad division point. All the freight trains stop there. Catch on?"

"So now we ride the rods," Sam said, in disgust.

"We don't have to. We can walk. I'd guess that it wasn't more than fourteen hundred and fifty miles to New York."

"We ride the rods. But what about food?"

"Tomorrow, pal. Tonight we travel."

8

FOURTH AVENUE, between Hennepin and Nicollet in Minneapolis, looked exactly like Market Street in St. Louis, West Madison in Chicago, and the Bowery in New York. The bums and hoboes congregated here by the hundreds and thousands. They gathered about the signs put out by the employment agencies, sat on the curb soaking up the sun and perhaps thinking of their lost years.

These streets always discouraged Johnny Fletcher. He'd been on them before and they were ever present, as horrible examples. He led Sam Cragg back to Hennepin and headed uptown.

Passing under the canopy of the Hennepin Theater, a man stepped out and beckoned to them. "You fellows," he said, sharply, "you want jobs?"

"Ha!" exclaimed Johnny. "Do we want

jobs? We do, Mister. What sort of jobs do you have?"

"What the hell do you care what the work is? You get paid two dollars at nine o'clock tonight."

"From now until nine tonight for two bucks?" Sam protested.

The man fell back. "Okay, wise guys, if that's the way you feel. . . . I can get a hundred men. . . ."

"We'll take the job!" Johnny said, smartly. "Lead on." The man led them into the darkened theater, where the ushers were just going through their morning drill. They went down a long tunnel, then climbed a short flight of stairs and were backstage. There their guide pointed to a door. "Your uniforms are in there. Be ready in five minutes."

"Uniforms?" Johnny Fletcher's nostrils flared. He pushed open the door and recoiled.

In the room were three gigantic caricatures of Pinocchio. Live caricatures. They wore huge shoes, short wool socks, had bare knees and above the knees short pantaloons with suspenders that covered flaming yellow shirts. Papier-mâché masks blessedly covered the wearer's faces and were surmounted by saucy little hats.

"No!" Johnny whispered.

One of the Pinocchios leered at them. "You the other chumps? There're your outfits."

"I won't," moaned Sam Cragg. "I won't go out in public wearing an outfit like that."

"That's what we said," another Pinocchio offered, "but two bucks is two bucks and they just threw off five thousand more men from the WPA."

Johnny stumbled into the room and from a chair picked up one of the costumes. He looked at Sam Cragg and a shudder ran through him. "How hungry are you, Sam?"

"Too hungry," Sam groaned. He began stripping off his coat.

They had scarcely finished dressing when Simon Legree, alias the manager of the theater, pounded on the door. "Come on, you Pinocchios, you're late."

Like condemned men the quintet of Pinocchios filed out of the dressing room. They followed the manager to the lobby of the theater, where he gave them their instructions.

"We're showing Walt Disney's *Pinocchio* this week, see," he said. "This is a publicity stunt to attract attention. The main thing to remember is to act like Pinocchios. Pinocchio was a lively youngster. He jumped and hopped and skipped. He was never still a moment. Catch on? I could use dummies just as well as you birds. . . . I'm paying you two bucks a day to move around. And remember, I'll be watching you. Now, go out there and give me a good day's work. You bring enough people into the theater and I may hire you all again tomorrow. Scram! . . ."

There was a small queue of ticket buyers already lined up before the ticket window when the Pinocchios finally reached the sidewalk. At sight of the

Pinocchios, passers-by on the sidewalk stopped.

"Oh, look!" a young thing exclaimed to her escort, a broad-faced Swede. "Aren't they cute!"

Cold sweat broke out all over Johnny Fletcher's body. A thick-bodied Pinocchio reeled against him. "God, what a man'll do when he's hungry!"

The manager of the theater came out and signaled to the Pinocchios. They shuffled over. "You're standing around like a bunch of dopes," he snapped. "Put some ginger into it or I'll fire the whole lot of you right away . . . and you can sue me for the wages. Go on, now!"

Back to the sidewalk they went. They did little jigs, stamped their feet and bobbed up and down. They played a game of leapfrog. And hundreds and hundreds of people stopped and blocked the sidewalks and the traffic on the street.

Policemen blew whistles and could not break the traffic snarl. After a while an emergency squad came and began regimenting the crowds. The manager of the theater stood beside the ticket office, a broad smile on his mean face as customers plunked down their money and bought tickets.

The Pinocchios played Ring Around the Rosie, London Bridge Is Falling Down and other little games that kept them moving about. They played until they were exhausted, then shuffled about on leaden feet until the manager came out and urged them on again. After two hours of it, he finally decided to let them rest in stretches of fifteen minutes each.

When it came Johnny's turn he staggered to the dressing room. There was no couch in the room but he stretched out on the floor. He was too tired even to remove his mask. He had been lying on the floor for ten minutes before he was aware that there was a folded newspaper in the small of his back. He rolled over and removed the paper. A headline caught his eye and he took off his mask and opened the door.

Most of the front page was devoted to the Brooklands affair. According to the paper, one Tom Quisenberry, aged twenty, had been strangled in the Brooklands Jail, by three tramps who called themselves, respectively: John Doe, John Smith and John Jones. John Doe, according to a statement made by Ora Fitch, the Brooklands constable, was a superannuated, feeble-minded bindle stiff. John Smith and John Jones, however, were young, vicious characters. They had attacked Fitch, the constable, and one or the other of them had stabbed him, inflicting a painful though not a serious wound.

A widespread police dragnet was out for the desperadoes and the state police expected to make an arrest shortly.

In another column was news of Diana Rusk. The former fiancee of Tom Quisenberry had been arrested the evening before near Moose Lake, after being seen with two men whose descriptions fitted those of Smith and Jones. The desperadoes had made their escape after a thrilling chase, but Diana Rusk had denied that the men in her car had been more than casual hitchhikers. The police, however, had held her until Eric Quisenberry, father of the murdered youth, who had just arrived from Hillcrest, New York, had interceded in her behalf.

Quisenberry, the paper went on to say, was taking the body of his son back to New York for burial, but before leaving had announced an offer of $1,000 for the capture of John Smith and John Jones.

"I've a good notion to claim that reward," Johnny said to himself. "I may never be worth that much money again."

"Hey, Pinocchio!" yelled a man outside the dressing room. "You've stayed over your time." The door was kicked in by an irate Pinocchio and Johnny picked himself up from the floor with a groan.

The day dragged on leaden feet. The five Pinocchios made merry, crowds stared at them, made audible comments and bought tickets. There was a line a half block long by mid-afternoon, trying to get into the theater, but still the Pinocchios were given no relief. They were allowed, one at a time, a half hour for lunch, but the manager vigorously resisted giving any advance on their salaries and Johnny and Sam had to content themselves with a nap for lunch.

Evening and nine o'clock came at long last. On the stroke of the hour, the five Pinocchios headed for the theater and the dressing room. Johnny and Sam had peeled off their costumes and donned their own clothing when the manager finally came with their wages.

"You be needing us tomorrow?" Johnny asked.

The manager fidgeted. "Why, uh, I don't think so. Maybe . . . later in the week."

"You said if we did a good job you'd hire us again tomorrow," complained one of the other Pinocchios.

"I know, but we had such a crowd today that there's sure to be an overflow tomorrow."

"Is that so," Sam Cragg said. "Well, in that case. . . ." He put his big hand in the manager's face and shoved so hard that the manager was hurtled back against the wall. By the time he bounced back, Sam and Johnny were at the door.

"Food!" cried Johnny.

"A nice, thick steak. . . ."

9

MINNEAPOLIS to Columbus on a dollar and thirty cents. Minneapolis to Chicago, two days in box cars, gondolas and the blind baggage; a loaf of bread and twenty cents worth of bologna.

Fifty cents for a square meal in South Chicago, then the highway to Indianapolis. One day by express truck, twenty cents for food. Highway 40 then to Columbus. One day and a loaf of bread.

In Columbus the first cop who spied them scowled and moved forward.

They ducked across the street and turning a corner, ran. When they had lost the policeman, Johnny said: "We've got seventy cents between us and it may be food out of our mouths, but we've got to get cleaned up. You look like a candidate for the House of David baseball team, Sam."

Sam Cragg rubbed his week-old stubble of beard. "You don't look so hot yourself, Johnny. They may charge us for a haircut instead of a shave. . . . We shouldn't have given up our razors to that rube constable in Minnesota."

"We shouldn't have even seen that fellow," Johnny said. "But we did and here we are. Let's get shaved."

"Where?"

Johnny looked to the left, where he could see the state capitol, then turned to the right. "Somewhere up here there ought to be a barber college."

Sam winced. "A barber college!"

"Well, we could go to the Deshler-Walleck, or the Neil House, but I don't think they'd welcome us, not the way we look right now. . . . Maybe later."

"No!" scowled Sam. "I couldn't stand that. . . ."

Johnny shook his head. "I must be losing my grip. I don't feel up to it myself. Ah! . . ." He pointed ahead. "The Capital Barber College."

The next half hour was agony. Johnny

drew a barber student who should never have left the farm. He had a bad habit of waving the razor in front of the customer's eyes before nicking out a chunk of skin. Finally, however, he finished and began sticking adhesive tape on Johnny's face.

"Will you have a nice massage, sir?" he murmured.

Johnny looked to see if he'd put the razor away, then he pushed the farmer barber away and sat up. "I'd like to give *you* a massage," he said, "with a fence rail."

Sam was already finished. His own butcher had put a long red cut along Sam's jaw.

Outside, Johnny took the pawn ticket from his pocket. "Well, we may as well learn the worst."

"What for?" Sam demanded. "Even if the kid got only a buck on whatever he pawned we couldn't get it out of hock."

Johnny shrugged. "Maybe so, but there're places where they buy pawn tickets. A pawnbroker only gives about one tenth of what the things worth. The scalper in between ought to give another tenth. Might as well take a look at the thing and get an idea. . . . This is the street, too. Ought to be about two blocks from here."

The pawnbroker was of the old school. He had the three gold balls hanging over the door and the sign on his window read: "Uncle Joe, The Friend In Need."

They went in. Uncle Joe was a sharp-eyed, smooth shaven young man of about twenty-eight or thirty. Johnny handed him the pawn ticket. "Here we are, Uncle Joe," he said brightly. "Let's see if you've been taking good care of the old heirloom."

The pawnbroker fingered the ticket. After a moment he said, "You got the money to redeem this?"

"The question," said Johnny, "is have you got the bauble?"

The young pawnbroker grunted. He went to the rear of the shop, passed through a door and was gone so long that

Johnny became restless. He yelled: "Hey, come on, don't keep us waiting all day."

The pawnbroker reappeared. He carried a strange-looking object in his arm . . . an object made of gold or merely gilded, about five inches square and about ten inches tall.

Sam Cragg exclaimed: "A clock!"

"What did you expect?" asked the pawnbroker.

"A clock," said Johnny. "And a mighty fine-looking clock it is. Umm . . . been in our family since my grandfather's time."

The pawnbroker set the clock on the counter and fumbled with a tag. "Uh-hmm," he said, "with the interest it comes to two sixty-four. Yep, two hundred and sixty-four dollars. I won't bother with the odd pennies."

Johnny groaned. "That much?"

"What d'you expect? You got two hundred on it."

"But sixty-four dollars interest. . . . I—I haven't got quite that much with me."

Uncle Joe looked at him severely.

"Then why'd you come in? If you can't redeem it. . . ."

"I expected to. It's just that—well, I thought maybe ten dollars interest. After all. . . ."

"You've got two hundred and ten dollars? It's a deal."

For once Johnny Fletcher was caught flat-footed "What? . . ." he stammered.

"I need money," Uncle Joe said, curtly. "I got too much tied up in stock. The hell with the interest. Two-ten and she's yours again. . . ."

"Why," said Johnny, "that's darned decent of you. And I'm going to take you up on that. Uh . . . just hold it here until tomorrow morning and I'll see. . . ."

"So! You ain't got two-ten. All right make it two hundred even. Exactly what I gave you on it. I need the money today."

"So do I," said Johnny. "As a matter of fact, I haven't got the money with me. I won't have it until tomorrow. So . . . just hang on until then. Eh?"

The pawnbroker picked up the omate clock and set it on the back shelf. Just as he did, the clock made a whirring, grinding noise. A tiny gold door at the top of the clock flew open and a golden mannikin popped out, bowed and . . . spoke!

"Five o'clock and the day is nearly done" the mannikin said in a singsongy metallic voice.

Sam Cragg's eyes were popping. Johnny too, was staring. He watched the mannikin bow again and pop back into his hole, the golden door closing upon him.

"I'm getting to like it, myself," said the pawnbroker. "If I didn't need the money . . . I'd just as soon keep it."

Johnny moistened his lips. "You can't! We—we'll be back tomorrow with the money."

He picked up the pawn ticket that the broker had laid on the counter and put it in his pocket.

When they reached the sidewalk, Sam Cragg whistled. "A talking clock, Johnny! Did you hear it?"

"No wonder Uncle Joe gave the Kid

two hundred bucks on it. . . . Why, did you see the jewels on the face? That clock's worth a good many times two hundred bucks . . . even if it didn't talk. I'll be—"

A man who had been leaning against a mailbox straightened and stepped in front of them. "Hi, boys," he said.

Johnny stopped. Beside him, Sam Cragg was breathing hoarsely.

The stranger was a heavy set, dark-complexioned man of about forty-five. A sardonic smile twisted his face. "I've been waiting for you."

"For who?" asked Johnny.

"Why," said the other, "for John Smith and John Jones. Catch on? Shall we go somewhere and talk it over?"

"Somewhere?"

"Oh," said the heavy-set man. "I'm only a private dick. Jim Partridge is the name. I've got a room in the Brownfield across the street. Shall we go over?"

"I don't like private dicks," Sam Cragg said, truculently.

"Well," said Jim Partridge, "if it comes

to that, do you like Headquarters dicks better? If you do . . ."

"We'll listen to you," said Johnny. "Come along, Sam."

The Brownfield was a second-rate hotel of eight floors. Partridge's room was on the top floor, the last room at the end of the corridor. He unlocked it and switched on a light inside, for the room opened on an airshaft.

He got a bottle of whisky from a dresser drawer and poured out about three fingers into a water tumbler. He held the glass out to Johnny, who shook his head. "I'm on the wagon this week."

Sam Cragg also refused and Partridge opened his mouth and dumped the stuff down his throat. He poured out four fingers more, and holding the glass, sat down in a rickety rocking chair. Sam Cragg leaned against the bathroom door and Johnny seated himself on the sagging bed.

"We're listening, Jim Partridge."

Jim Partridge nodded. "To make a short story even shorter I want the pawn ticket you swiped from young Tom Quisenberry up there in Minnesota. That's all I want."

Johnny pursed up his lips. "Since you like it short, the answer is—uh-uh!"

"I thought you'd say that," replied Partridge. "All right. I'll play it your way. Old Simon Quisenberry shoved off yesterday. The Kid went off before the old man—so the clock reverts to the estate. I'm representing the estate."

"Tom's father, Eric Quisenberry?"

"The estate," repeated Jim Partridge. "Now, I don't think you boys are any mysterious strangers. I think you're just a couple of above-the-average bo's down on your luck. You just happened to be in that can when the boy was yowling. You saw a good thing and you took advantage of it. But . . . it's no soap. So, come across, boys."

Johnny locked his hands behind his head and leaned back on the bed. He looked up at the dirty ceiling. "Well, maybe we will, Partridge. But just to satisfy my curiosity, tell me some more about yourself. How'd you know the clock was in the pawnshop across the street?"

Partridge grunted. "I guess you haven't been around much. I'm pretty good in my line. Although I'll admit the Kid didn't leave much of a trail. It took me a month to trace him this far."

"A month?"

"Oh, sure. I've been tracing the Kid ever since he left home and the old man discovered he'd taken the clock with him."

"But last week the authorities of that Minnesota town got in touch with his family. How come you didn't hop to Minnesota?"

"I was after the clock, not the boy. He didn't have it with him up there."

"You weren't up in Brooklands, Minnesota, at all?"

Partridge smiled ironically. "Was I supposed to be up there? . . . You came right here, to me."

"That's right. How'd you know we would?"

"I read the papers. After you bumped the boy, you burned the roads getting away from there. That meant you had the ticket. . . . But what took you so long?"

"It was a tough road. Well, I've made up my mind, Partridge."

The private detective drained his glass and set it on the edge of the dresser. He leaned forward. "Let's have it."

"I made up my mind," Johnny said deliberately. "No."

Jim Partridge twitched. His hand went under his coat lapel, came out with a .38 automatic. He grinned. "I made up my mind—yes."

Johnny Fletcher sat up. The pillow he had gripped in both hands came up with him, sailed over his head—simultaneously with the water glass Sam Cragg had picked up from inside the bathroom and was hurling at Jim Partridge.

The pillow distracted Partridge and the water tumbler hit his jaw and smashed with a pop and shatter. Partridge gasped and fell forward out of the rocking chair.

"Nice teamwork," said Johnny leaping up.

Sam Cragg scooped up the .38 from the floor, where it had fallen from Partridge's limp hand. Partridge squirmed and moaned. Johnny straightened him out. "You didn't break his jaw, Sam," he said, "but he'll be drinking soup for a few days. . . . Throw the gun in the bathroom. We don't want to be bothered with it. Come on! . . ."

At the first street corner, Johnny bought a newspaper and stepped into a convenient doorway. "I think it's about time we caught up on the Quisenberry family. If that bird, Partridge, wasn't lying about Old Simon Quisenberry dying, there ought to be something in this about him—and the family."

He found it on Page 2, almost an entire column, under the heading:

GRANDFATHER OF MURDERED YOUTH SUCCUMBS

Johnny's eyes skimmed through the story.

Stripped of verbiage, it told simply that Simon Quisenberry, wealthy manufacturer of the famous Simple Simon Clocks, had died at his Hillcrest, New York, home, after a lengthy illness. The account hinted that his passing might have been accelerated by the shocking news of the murder of his grandson, Tom Quisenberry, several days previously while a prisoner in a Minnesota prison.

There was a brief resume of Simon Quisenberry's life. His hobby was touched upon for two paragraphs. Simon Quisenberry had invested a fortune in rare and unusual clocks; his collection was said to be the most valuable in existence, numbering among it many famous timepieces. The prize of his collection was a talking clock, for which Simon Quisenberry had once refused fifty thousand dollars.

Johnny Fletcher whistled when he came to that. "Fifty grand! And the Kid hocked it for two hundred bucks. I only hope that pawnbroker doesn't read this. He's liable to go south with the clock."

Sam Cragg sniffed. "That's a lot of malarkey. No clock's worth fifty G's. They always exaggerate those things. Like guys who get held up. They squawk to the cops that they were robbed of two bucks in cash and a diamond ring worth at least two thousand—and two grand isn't hay."

"It might as well be, for all the good it'd do us. We haven't got two hundred bucks and we probably never will have. Not in this town. I'm for heading back to little old Broadway, right now."

"Me, too, but we've got to find that girl, first. I told her we'd be here."

"How you going to find her in a town this size?"

"She'll be at a hotel, won't she? There are only four or five big hotels in the main part of town. She'll be at one of them."

Sam scowled. "And she'll have six cops in her room, ready to grab us. Anyway, why should we give her the clock—I mean, the pawn ticket? The Kid's got a family, hasn't he?"

"A father. But you'll remember he took

his time getting up to Minnesota. And the boy said his father had kicked him out. I think I'll just give the ticket to the girl. I have a hunch the Kid would have wanted it to go to her."

"I don't see why we have to give it to anyone. You said something about selling the ticket to some scalper for a couple of hundred...."

Johnny Fletcher looked steadily at his friend and Sam Cragg began to redden. "Well, I don't see anything worse in that than some of the things you've pulled at one time or another."

Johnny shook his head sadly. "Necessity has now and then compelled me to clip some corners a little sharp, Sam, but have you ever known me to rob a dead man . . . a dead boy?"

Sam sighed. "Okay, Johnny. Let's get rid of the ticket and start walking. There's the Deshler-Walleck; maybe she's staying there."

She wasn't, but she was registered at the second hotel where they inquired, the Neil House. Johnny considered for a moment going up to her room, then decided against it. Instead he got a sheet of paper and an envelope at the desk and wrote a brief note. He enclosed the pawn ticket with the note and sealing the envelope left it at the desk.

Then he turned to Sam. "All right, my boy, let's start that walking now. It's six hundred miles to Times Square."

10

"NEW YORK," said Johnny Fletcher. "I don't know why I ever leave it."

"I know why," said Sam Cragg sarcastically, "but I won't tell."

Johnny reached forward and tapped the driver of the sedan on the shoulder. "You make a left turn here and go straight through to the express highway over there."

"Thanks," said the driver. "Any special place I should let you off? And d'you know a good hotel me and the missus can stay at reasonable?"

"Yes," said Johnny. "The 45th Street Hotel. The manager's a personal friend—"

"Friend?" cried Sam Cragg.

"Friend," repeated Johnny, firmly. "You ask for Mr. Peabody and tell him Johnny Fletcher sent you and if he doesn't treat you right, why—" he chuckled—"why, I'll come and check in myself for a few weeks. That'll hold him. . . . And you can let us off right here, Mister."

The Iowan, who was coming to see the World's Fair, pulled over to the curb. Johnny and Sam climbed out and shook hands with the driver and his wife.

"Folks," Johnny said, gratefully, "we sure appreciate this lift you've given us all the way for Chambersburg."

"Oh, that's all right," said the Iowan's wife. "If you ever come through Shell Rock, Iowa, stop in and say hello. Everyone there knows us—the August Schultz's."

"Nice people," said Johnny when the car with the Iowa plates had pulled on. "And now—let's see if the old town's changed any."

"The cops will be tougher with the fair going on," Sam said, sourly.

"I like 'em tough," Johnny said. "That's why I like New York. She's always tough and I'm at my best when the goings tough. Well, let's go see Mort Murray first of all."

"Yeah," said Sam, a gleam coming into his eye. "We'll ask him how come he sent those books to Poplar City, Minnesota, express collect. That's what started all our troubles."

Twenty minutes later they turned into West Seventeenth Street and paused before a pre-Civil War loft building. Johnny regarded it fondly. "And from this moment on, our troubles are over."

They entered the building and climbed four flights of stairs for there was no elevator in the place. On the fourth floor landing Johnny turned toward a door. With his hand on the knob, he groaned.

"What's this paper on the door?" he snapped.

"An eviction notice!" Sam Cragg yelped. "Why the dirty.... They can't do this to us!"

"They didn't do it to us," Johnny said, sadly. "They did it to poor Old Mort. No wonder he sent us those books collect. He was strapped. Damn a big express company that doesn't trust an honest man for a dollar or two."

Johnny jiggled the doorknob and even tried kicking the door. It was firmly locked. He tore the eviction notice from the door and read it. "For a lousy eighty bucks—two months' rent!" he snorted. "Why, they ought to be glad they can get even a non-paying tenant for this rat's nest."

He threw the sheet of paper to the floor and started for the stairs.

"Now, what'll we do?" Sam wailed. "Mort was our only chance. Even if he couldn't give us any dough, he'd a come across with some books. He never failed us like this."

"That just goes to show. Mort's one of these honest guys. He pays his bills and they get in the habit of expecting money from him, so when he doesn't come across what do they do? They lock him out—Hey! . . ."

They were coming down the final flight of stairs as a mournful-looking man in a seedy suit opened the door. He was in his early thirties, needed a shave and his bare head was a shock of black hair combed in a rough pompadour. Mort Murray could have posed for a cartoonist who wanted to draw a caricature of a Union Square orator.

"Mort!"

Mort Murray's mouth fell open. "Johnny Fletcher! Sam Cragg! . . ." He sprang forward to meet Johnny and threw his arms about him with the fervor of a man who's just been saved by an evangelist.

"Jeez, Mort!" cried Johnny Fletcher. "What'd they do to you, the dirty rats?"

Mort stepped back and there was moisture in his eyes. "The going's been tough, fellas. They threw my stepfather off the WPA, and I've been afraid to even go around to my mother's place. You know, she used to slip me a buck now and then. Why, last night—" Mort's voice broke with self-pity. "Why last night I hadda sleep on the subway!"

Johnny shook his head in sympathy. He forgot that he and Sam Cragg, for the last two weeks, would have been glad of a friendly, sheltered subway to sleep in. "No wonder you had to send those books express collect up to Minnesota!"

Mort Murray winced. "I never let you down before, boys, did I? I hope it didn't inconvenience you. . . ."

"Hell, no!" said Johnny.

"Hell, no!" said Sam Cragg. "All it did was get us thrown in jail. And we've practically starved ever since—but don't give it a second thought, Mort."

"Tsk, tsk!" said Johnny. "Everything'll be all right now, Mort. Look, we're stony. But don't let that worry you. You've got a few books that aren't locked upstairs?"

Mort Murray drooped. "Not a book, Johnny. They caught me by surprise. If I'd only known . . ."

Johnny scowled and bit his lips. "How about the windows?"

"They open on a courtyard and besides—there are bars on them."

"Damn, that makes it tough. Who's your landlord?"

"The Sailor's Safe Seaport. They own all the real estate around here. You know how they are."

'The toughest! All these charitable institutions are tough. Well, look, give them a ring. Ask them how much they'll take on account to open up."

"How'll I call them? Uh . . . either of you got a nickel?"

Johnny looked at Sam. The latter scowled. "You know I haven't."

"All right," said Johnny. "How about the Italian Delicatessen across the street? Does he know you well enough to let you use his phone?"

"It's a pay phone." Mort winced. "I owe him a couple of bucks now."

"Then a nickel more or less won't matter. Come on. . . ."

They left the loft building and crossed the street to the delicatessen. "Hello Tony," Mort greeted the proprietor, cheerfully. "Can I use your phone?"

"Sure," said Tony, sourly. "You put in the nickel and make the dial."

Johnny took command. "Look, Tony,

Mort's broke and I forgot my money at home. . . . I left it on the piano. Mort wants to call up his uncle and ask him for twenty dollars. His uncle's captain of the 44th Precinct, you know. Now, be a good fellow and let Mort have a nickel. Then when he gets the twenty he'll pay you those couple of dollars he owes you. Thanks, pal!"

Tony glared at Johnny Fletcher but punched the No Sale on his cash register and produced a nickel. Mort took it and went into the telephone booth. He was inside for three minutes, then came out perspiring.

"Okay, Mort?"

Mort shook his head.

"How much do they want?"

"A hundred and twenty dollars."

"But you only owe them eighty!"

"I know, but another month's rent is due next week and they say they won't unlock unless I pay that too. . . . I even told them I was an old-time sailor, but it didn't work."

Johnny began swearing. Sam Cragg

joined in, but Mort Murray was too discouraged for even that bit of relief. Tony, the delicatessen man, came around from behind his counter.

"Look Meester Murray," he said, "you needing one hundred twenny dollar?"

"I won't need it in heaven."

"You got beezness, Meester Murray," said Tony. "Theese friend—they are customer, maybe?"

"The best I ever had. But they can't work unless I give them some books. And I've got other orders for books. They're piled up, but they're all credit orders..."

"Well, Meester Murray," said Tony. "I feex him for you. I getting you the money."

"What?" cried Johnny Fletcher. "You're going to lend Mort the money?"

"Me? Who you t'ink I am? Rockyfeller, maybe? No, I got brudder-in-law; he give you the money. Wait, I calling him on the telephone...."

He went into the phone booth, closed the door and came out in a half minute.

"He be right here. I catching him in the pool room around the corner. Carmella, he giving you the money."

Carmella came strolling into the delicatessen in a few minutes. He was a slit-eyed, olive skinned man of about thirty. He wore an expensive pin-striped suit and had a diamond pin stuck in his flaming red tie.

"Hello, boys," he said, smoothly. "Hear you need a little money."

"A loan shark!" exclaimed Johnny.

Carmella regarded Johnny calmly. "The name is Carmella Genualdi. I work for Julius, just so you won't make any mistake. Now, which one of you is it wants the money?"

A little shiver ran through Mort Murray. "M-me. A hundred and twenty dollars."

Carmella looked at his brother-in-law, the delicatessen man. The latter bobbed his head up and down. "He gotting the business 'cross the street. Book, or something."

Carmella took a thick roll from his

trousers pocket, took off the rubber band and counted off five twenty-dollar bills. "Since you're a friend of Tony's, I'll give you a break, on the interest. It'll be ten dollars a day. You won't owe any interest until Wednesday. One of the boys'll be around to collect it . . . every day."

"Say, isn't that pretty steep interest?" asked Johnny.

"It's more'n the bank'd charge," said Carmella. "But can any of you birds borrow money at a bank?" He smiled thinly at Mort. "And don't forget, we like our interest paid prompt. Huh?" Without waiting for a reply he nodded and left the store.

"Brr!" Johnny shuddered. "Nice relations you got, Tony."

"Oh, sure, Carmella's all right. He's out on, what you call? The bail? He's breaking fella's arm, last week."

"Let's get out of here," said Sam Cragg.

"Hey!" cried Tony. "You paying me the two dollar forty cent you owe? . . ."

"Tomorrow," said Johnny. Mort's got

to save for the interest to pay your brother-in-law. Come on, Mort."

Outside he said to Mort, "Now, let's run over to this sailors outfit. We'll give them eighty bucks and if they don't take it, I'll choke it down the admiral's sanctimonious throat."

"That's the stuff, Johnny," said Sam Cragg. He smacked his lips. "I feel better already. Our troubles are over. Yours, too, Mort. Which reminds me . . . uh . . ." He took the handkerchief and cards from his pocket. "Ever see the old handkerchief trick, Mort?"

"What?" exclaimed Mort. *"You* taking up magic?"

Johnny grunted. "It'd be magic if his tricks ever worked."

Sam ignored Johnny. He draped the handkerchief across his arm, fanned out his pack of cards and said, "Take a card, Mort. . . . That's fine. Now put it back here."

He shuffled the cards and then took the handkerchief and spread it out on his right palm. With his left hand, he placed the pack of cards in the center of the handkerchief. He started to fold the handkerchief over the cards, then muttered: "No, I don't do it that way. Let's see . . . I got to double the handkerchief first . . ." He uncovered the cards, fumbled the pack and it fell to the sidewalk.

"Is that the trick, Sam?" cried Mort.

"That's it, Mort," said Johnny. "The idea is to see how far you can scatter the cards. . . . Come on, let's get this rent business cleaned up. I feel nice and mean."

11

As they left the restaurant Mort Murray shook hands with both Sam and Johnny. "Look, fellas, I ain't worried about Carmella at all. Only . . ."

"Sure, Mort," said Johnny, soothingly. "You can count on me. I'm going right out with these books now. Tomorrow morning when you come down to your office at nine o'clock we'll be waiting for you. With some dough."

"I'll bet," said Sam, sotto voce. He picked up a carton in each hand, carrying them as if they weighed four or five pounds instead of forty.

Mort shook hands all around again and trotted back to his office. Johnny and Sam headed for Fourteenth Street.

Johnny looked down Fourteenth Street. "There's a cop up the street. Besides, I worked here once before. Let's see, where else can I get a crowd without the damn cops breaking it up before they reach for the folding money?"

"How about the World's Fair?"

Johnny scowled. "No pitchmen, even if we could afford the tax. . . . Jeez, did you ever see so many cops in New York? Must be the fair. I'll tell you what, we've got a couple of bucks, why not run out to one of the better suburbs?"

"Where?" Sam howled.

Johnny screwed up his face. "Oh, maybe White Plains or Scarsdale. Or perhaps . . ."

"Don't tell me! Hillcrest!"

"Why, yes, that's a nice town. . . ."

"I knew it! You've had this in mind all the time. The clock girl lives in Hillcrest. You want to stick your nose into that business. Well, I don't. I'm perfectly satisfied to be out of it and I'm going to stay out of it. You wouldn't get me out to Hillcrest if you put me in a straitjacket. . . ."

So they went to the Grand Central and rode out to Hillcrest. Arriving there,

Johnny went into a store to ask directions. He came out after a moment, a strange look on his face.

He said to Sam: "Let's jump into that cab there. It's a kind of long walk...."

"To where?"

"You'll see.... Taxi!"

He let Sam pile into the taxicab with the cartons containing their supplies, then before climbing in himself leaned over into the driver's compartment and gave him a direction.

The taxi made a U turn, cut across traffic and zoomed up a winding street. Houses and trees rushed by and after a few minutes the driver slammed on the brake of the taxi and said, "Fifty cents, gents!"

"A cemetery!" Sam howled. "What the?..."

"They're burying Simon Quisenberry," Johnny said, defensively. "He was the Mr. Big of Hillcrest and the whole town's turned out, including the folks we want to see."

"I don't like cemeteries," Sam

protested. "If I never see one that's soon enough for me. Let's get out of here. You're not going to get me into anything, Johnny. I won't stand for it."

"Shut up, Sam!" Johnny paid the taxi driver and headed up the graveled drive into the cemetery. Ahead was a vast throng of people. That the entire town of Hillcrest had turned out was an exaggeration, but not too much so. There were fully five hundred people in the cemetery.

Johnny left Sam behind and began skirting the edge of the throng. In the center the proceedings were going on and he was vaguely aware of a voice droning through the burial ritual. Johnny, however, was not interested in Simon Quisenberry. He was dead and was of no further consequence. Some day Johnny would die and he would cease to be of importance to anyone.

He sought a living face, a girl's. But, although he circled the entire crowd once and peered at every young woman's face, he saw none that he could recognize. Sam, meanwhile, had set his heavy cartons on the ground and seated himself on one of them.

Through a break, Johnny saw the figure of the portly mortician, in swallow tail and striped trousers, who seemed to be presiding over the ceremony. His voice came, sonorously:

"Is there anyone here who would like to say a few words before we consign the mortal remains of the deceased to the earth from which he sprung?"

There was no response. No sound of weeping. Johnny was suddenly struck by that. He had seen no tear-stained or grief-stricken faces in his circuit of the crowd. Many had come to see Simon Quisenberry lowered into his grave, but none had come to mourn.

Johnny wheeled and hurried over to Sam. "Pick up the boxes and hurry down to the gate, Sam."

"What?" gasped Sam. "You aren't thinking?—"

"I am," Johnny said, tersely. "None of these people are mourning. Maybe they're thinking of the Great Beyond, but that's fine. They're in a soft mood—for us. Come on. . . ."

Already people were moving away, going to the limousines and other cars, or walking toward the gate below. Before one of them passed through the gate, however, Johnny was standing on one of the cartons and Sam was on the other, peeling off his coat.

He was stripping down his shirt when the vanguard arrived, blinking and murmuring at the strange sight.

Johnny threw up his hands in oratorical manner and his voice boomed out. "Ladies and gentlemen, give me your attention a moment. You have just come from burying our beloved fellow citizen, Simon Quisenberry. You have paid your last respects to the dead and now you return . . . to the living. But before you go, I have a message for you. All you who are alive and well today.

"One day, you too will be carried through this gate. Let us hope, however, that will not be for many years. And it need not be, ladies and gentlemen. It need not be for many, many years. It will not be—if you live moderate, temperate lives . . . and watch your health.

"Your health, ladies and gentlemen. Which is the same as saying your life. I want you to take a look at my friend here. . . ." He reached out and slapped Sam Cragg's chest with his palm. "Look at him. Isn't he the most marvelous physical specimen you ever saw? Look at his rippling muscles, his tremendous chest. Wonderful, isn't it? Yet. . . ."

Johnny's voice fell to a hush, which nevertheless carried a hundred feet. "Yet . . . one day, not so many years ago, this wonderful body was a mere shell. It was wracked with disease. This man here before you, weighing 220 pounds of muscle and bone and wonderful health, was a mere shadow. He weighed 96 pounds and the finest doctors in the country gave him but six months to live. . . ."

The exodus from the cemetery had halted. The pedestrians had blocked the exit and the drivers of the automobiles hesitated about blowing their horns. You didn't blow a horn in a cemetery. So they stood in the graveled drive, a line of cars, surrounded by hundreds of people. By the gate, Johnny Fletcher went on with his spiel. As he talked, he took a strong web belt that Sam handed to him and buckled it tightly about Sam's chest.

His voice rang out: "He came to me, puny, dying on his feet. He said, 'The docs have given me up. I've heard about your secret body-building methods. I've got nothing to lose. Try them on me. I don't think they'll work, but if they do . . .' He left it up to me. He would not blame me if I failed. But did I fail? . . . Look at him, now! Ladies and gentlemen, look at Young Samson, the strongest man in the world. Look at his powerful body, his glowing face, his wonderful health. . . . Look at him! . . ." His voice rose to a screaming pitch, as Sam, drawing a deep breath, expanded his chest.

There was a sudden hush and in the midst of it, a loud pop. The web belt about Sam's chest snapped and flew away from his body.

"Did you see that?" Johnny Fletcher thundered. "Did you see him break that strong web belt with a mere expansion of his chest? Is there any man in this crowd strong enough to do such a thing? No! Of course not. Because none of you have had access to my secrets of body building. But wait . . . in just a moment . . ."

Johnny leaped down from his box, tore it open and brought out a six-foot length of heavy iron chain. He held it aloft. "Do you see this chain, ladies and gentlemen? It is made of strong iron links, forged by a master smith. It is known as a logging chain, used by lumberjacks to haul heavy timbers. Sometimes it is used in a block and tackle to raise and lower iron safes or building stones. Watch me closely, now, ladies and gentlemen. Watch me. . . ."

He stepped up on his box again and began putting the chain around Sam's body. He brought the ends together in front of Sam, pulled them taut and twisted them together. . . .

As he worked, a voice in the front of the crowd said audibly: "What's the man going to do? Who is he, anyway? . . ."

"Here in the cemetery . . ." said another voice.

A woman's voice rose shrilly: "This is sacrilege!"

People began milling, forging through the gates. Johnny saw the crowd become restless and threw up his hands again: "Wait just one moment more, folks. Watch Young Samson, the strongest man in all the world, break that chain that is twisted about his body. Watch him perform a feat of strength that none of you have ever seen before or will ever see again. Watch this living miracle, who was once a puny weakling. . . ."

A perspiring village policeman, urged forward by a woman, broke through the front rank of the crowd and advanced upon Johnny. "Here you, what are you trying to do? Who are you, anyway? . . ."

"A public benefactor!" howled Johnny. "That's who I am. Years ago I discovered certain secret principles of life, health.

I've devoted my time ever since to making these secrets accessible to all . . . so that humanity may benefit by them. Yes, even you, Officer, can benefit. You're a well-built man, strong, and you look healthy. But can you perform the feat of strength my friend has just exhibited? Can you? Yes, you can. . . . How? Why, merely by reading a book I'm going to make available to you in a moment. A book called *Every Man a Samson*, which contains all of the secrets, exercises and formulas that Young Samson had to study to become what he is . . ."

"A book salesman!" the policeman exclaimed, hoarsely. "Why, you!"

"Watch!" Johnny roared. "Watch Young Samson break this chain. Watch him! . . ."

Sam lowered himself several inches, spread his feet apart and drew a deep breath. He let it out slowly, rising at the same time. His muscles became cords, his face reddened from tremendous exertion and perspiration streamed down his face.

The iron links of the chain cut into his flesh . . . and every person within sight watched. . . .

Up . . . up. . . . The veins stood out on Sam's throat like ropes, his face turned almost black. . . .

And then the chain snapped!

A link broke and the chain flew away from Sam and missed the policeman by less than three inches. It landed on the ground, plain for all in front to see the link, pulled out of shape, broken! . . .

And now Johnny was down from the carton, tearing it open and piling books into his arms.

"Here it is, ladies and gentlemen! *Every Man a Samson*, the book that tells you how to become as strong and healthy as Young Samson, whom you have just observed. The secrets of life, vitality. . . . health. . . . Just $2.95! . . ."

He attacked the crowd with a vigor that was in keeping with the amazing things that had happened during the last few minutes. Behind him came Sam, still perspiring, still red in the face, but books piled up in his muscular arms. He was passing them out right and left, taking money in his powerful hands, rippling the muscles in his arms and shoulders for all to see at close range.

People milled about, murmured, chattered . . . and above it all thundered Johnny Fletcher's voice, exhorting, pleading, urging. . . . "Two dollars and ninety-five cents! A paltry two dollars and ninety-five cents for added years of life. You can save the amount in pills and medicines, doctor's bills, over and over. Two dollars and . . ."

The crowd dispersed, automobiles were able to roll through the gates and go down into Hillcrest. People followed. Inside of ten minutes, there was only a sprinkling of them left.

Johnny Fletcher kicked one of the cartons, discovered that it was empty and tossed a couple of books into the second carton.

"Not bad, Sam, not bad at all. . . ."

Sam said, out of the side of his mouth,

"That man is still here." He stooped and scooped up his shirt and coat.

"Look here, you two," the village policeman said, in a bewildered, yet determined voice. "You can't do a thing like that. Why, you're nothing but book salesmen and coming here to a cemetery like this . . ."

Johnny clapped hands together. "Did I miss you? Of course! Well, Officer, here it is. One copy of *Every Man a Samson*. And—no, no! I refuse to take any money from you. . . . It's yours, sir, absolutely free. Without charge of any kind. With the compliments of myself and Young Samson. . . ."

The policeman took the book, flushed and frowned. He ended by throwing up his hands, "Aw, hell!"

Johnny chuckled. "Ain't it?"

The policeman fingered the copy of *Every Man a Samson*. "But don't do it again, Mister. Not in Hillcrest. We got a local ordinance about street peddlers and the merchants and Chamber of Commerce raise hell. They say it takes money out of Hillcrest. . . ."

"Sure, Officer. Now, I wonder if you could direct us to the estate of the late Simon Quisenberry?"

12

IT was a formidable iron gate and Joe Cornish, when he came out of the gate house in response to Johnny Fletcher's ring, looked even more formidable than the gate.

He examined Johnny and Sam and was apparently not impressed with what he saw, for he said, surlily:

"What do you want?"

"I want to see Mr. Eric Quisenberry, my good man," Johnny replied loftily. "Will you be so good as to unlock this gate?"

"Quisenberry isn't seeing people," Cornish replied, curtly. "And I'm not your good man."

"Ha! Well, trot into that hole of yours and telephone the house. Tell Mr. Quisenberry that a gentleman wants to see him . . . about Uncle Joe, in Columbus, Ohio."

"Quisenberry hasn't got any relatives in Ohio. What're you trying to pull?"

Johnny gripped the iron bars of the gate and peered through. "Who are you—one of the poor relatives? If you aren't, get on that telephone and be damned quick about it!"

"Before I climb over and knock your teeth down your throat," Sam Cragg muttered.

Cornish regarded Johnny sullenly for a moment, then shrugged and went into his cottage. When he came out, he unbolted the gate.

"I'll be waiting here when you come back," he said, significantly.

"Swell," retorted Sam.

As they started up the drive, Johnny exclaimed, "Look, the place is laid out like a clock; one walk for each hour. This Quisenberry guy certainly liked his clocks."

"Where he's gone now, he won't need no clocks," Sam retorted, philosophically. "And if this Eric Quisenberry guy is half as smart as I think he is, we won't be needing any either—not for a good many years."

"Always the pessimist, aren't you, Sam? Shucks, Quisenberry ought to know by now that we didn't kill his son." He added under his breath, "I hope."

Eric Quisenberry came out of the house as they approached the veranda. He was wearing rough tweeds and standing with his feet spread apart, said crisply:

"You're the men from Columbus?"

"We've been there," said Johnny. "Minnesota, too."

"Ah!" exclaimed Eric Quisenberry. "Then you must be John Smith—"

"That's right, and this is my friend, John Jones."

Quisenberry grunted. "We'll let the names slide for the moment. Do you claim to be the men who gave Miss Rusk a certain ticket?"

"A pawn ticket. For the Talking Clock. She redeemed it okay?"

Quisenberry relaxed "She gave it to me last night. She told me about you, too, but I'll be frank with you. I don't understand. If you're—well, *were* you with my son, Tom, in that jail?"

Johnny nodded. "We spent one night there. But we didn't kill him. That's what I came here to tell you. There was another man in that jail. He was there, with Tom, for several hours before we were thrown in . . ."

"What'd he look like?"

Johnny shrugged. "He looked like the worst tramp you'd ever set eyes on. Yet —during the night, Tom crept to my bed and forced that pawn ticket into my hand. Apparently he was afraid of this fourth man. In the morning . . ." He paused and looked curiously at Eric Quisenberry.

Quisenberry nodded. "Go ahead. I want to get it all."

"In the morning, Tom was dead. The constable came to wake us and this fourth man—the tramp—pulled a knife, slashed at the constable and darted out. We followed. . . ."

"Why? If you were innocent?"

"We acted on impulse. Frankly, we were in that jail for vagrancy. We'd had a series of misfortunes and we were stony broke. With the tramp making a clean getaway, it struck me that we'd be the goats . . . accused of everything and little or no chance to disprove the charge."

"I talked to that constable—Fitch, or whatever his name is. He seemed pretty certain you, or—" Quisenberry glanced at Sam—"your partner had committed . . . had killed Tim. . . ."

Behind him, Bonita Quisenberry came to the door. "Excuse me, Eric," she said. "Cornish just telephoned from the gate. He's sending up the Greek."

Bonita Quisenberry looked from Johnny to Sam, then came out to the veranda. Johnny heard an automobile coming up the drive, in second gear. He turned and watched the long coupe slide up in front of the veranda.

A tall, olive-skinned man of about forty climbed out. "Hallo, Mr. Quisenberry," he said.

"Hello, Bos," Quisenberry said, shortly. "What can I do for you?"

Nicholas Bos showed strong, white

teeth. "I am sorry to be so impatient, but I am come . . . alas, I am come for the clock."

"You didn't waste any time, did you?" Bonita Quisenberry said, sharply.

Her husband frowned at her. "Father did tell us, my dear . . ." he murmured.

"Yes," Bonita said, witheringly, "he told us about the Talking Clock, too. *That* isn't included?"

"Begging pardon," Nicholas Bos said, quickly. "You . . . have obtained the Talking Clock?"

"We have," Mrs. Quisenberry said, "And I may as well tell you right now, that a certain clock collector in Toronto has made us a very nice offer on it. . . ."

"No! You cannot sell. Simon want me having it . . ."

"If you'll pay for it!"

A cloud passed across the olive-skinned man's face. He bowed stiffly. "You will permitting examine clock?"

"I guess it'll be all right," said Eric Quisenberry, looking at his wife. She nodded.

Uninvited, Johnny moved toward the door. Quisenberry bumped against him and paused. "My dear," he murmured to his wife, "I forgot to introduce Mr. Smith . . . and Mr. Jones. And Mr. Nicholas Bos, gentlemen."

"Smith," said Bonita Quisenberry, "and Jones. Not the—"

"Of the Smiths and Joneses," Johnny said, grinning. "We're the bright lads who retrieved the old Talking Clock. We didn't get a good look at it before. D'you mind?"

Bonita Quisenberry looked coldly at Johnny. "What's your angle? Diana seemed to be taken in by you, but as for me, I'm convinced—"

"Tut-tut," said Johnny. "Would we be here, if we had?"

"I don't know," Bonita retorted bluntly. "There are a lot of things I don't like about this business."

"Why, that's just what I was thinking. . . . Shall we?" Johnny bowed toward the door.

Bonita went into the house. The others

followed through a wide hall into a living room, then into a pine-paneled room, about twenty feet square. Stepping into the room, Johnny stopped. Behind him, Sam Cragg whistled.

There were more clocks in this room than in a clock store. And what clocks they were! Big clocks, little clocks and medium-sized clocks. There were clocks made of metal and wood, of stone and marble. Grandfather clocks and tiny table models. They were of all colors, shapes and designs. Gold and silver gleamed, brass and bronze shone.

And all the clocks were ticking. Pendulums swung, wheels whirred.

Eric Quisenberry went to a panel, pressed, and a wooden door swung open, revealing the black steel door of a wall safe. He manipulated the dial a moment then pulled open the door. He reached in and brought out the Talking Clock, setting it down on a table in the middle of the room.

Nicholas Bos said: "Ah!" His eyes were shining with avarice.

"It's two minutes to three o'clock," said Eric Quisenberry. "In two minutes it will talk."

Nicholas Bos ran his hands lovingly over the clock. "Yes," he murmured, "it is the Talking Clock I must have it."

"How much?" demanded Bonita Quisenberry.

Nicholas Bos raised his eyes to Mrs. Quisenberry's face. "Fifty t'ousand dollar, I will giving."

"Come again!"

Nicholas Bos swallowed hard. "How much this Canada man say he pay?"

"More than fifty thousand," retorted Bonita.

"Horace Potter don't have more," said Bos, bluntly. "I don't believing."

Bonita's nostrils flared. "You're calling me a liar?" she cried, shrilly.

Bos threw up his hands as if to ward her off. "No, no, Madame. I—is just business term. You trying get more money. I say no."

Bonita turned to her husband. "You

going to let him get away with that, Eric?"

Quisenberry cleared his throat. He was visibly embarrassed and Johnny guessed then who it was wore the pants in the Quisenberry family.

Quisenberry said, "Look here, Mr. Bos! . . ."

And then pandemonium took over in the clock room.

It was three o'clock and every blessed clock in the room, hundreds of them, sounded off. Cuckoos came out of their holes, and cuckooed. Bells rang, horns tooted, chimes chimed and clappers banged on gongs.

Startled almost out of his wits, Johnny tried to keep his eyes on the Talking Clock. He saw the little gold man come out, bow, but his words were drowned out by the hideous racket of the other clocks. Nicholas Bos, however, put his ear right down beside the little gold man who had come out of the Talking Clock. An expression of stupefaction came over his face.

It was only three o'clock, so the hundreds of clocks were soon finished with their tasks. Johnny wondered what the inhabitants of this house did at noon or midnight. . . . They probably ducked for the cellar.

With the echoes of the racket dying out, Nicholas Bos straightened.

"All right," he announced. "I will giving you seventy-five thousand dollars."

"Now you're beginning to talk our language," Bonita Quisenberry exclaimed. "What do you say, Eric? . . ."

Eric Quisenberry coughed. "I think, Mr. Bos, you've made a deal. Yes sir, if you're prepared to pay cash, I think we can arrange—"

"Aren't you forgetting something?" Johnny Fletcher interposed softly. "According to what I read in the papers, this Talking Clock was bequeathed by Simon Quisenberry to his grandson Tom."

"I know that," Eric Quisenberry said, frowning. "But since I am his father, the clock naturally devolves—"

"Perhaps," said Johnny. "And perhaps not."

Bonita Quisenberry stepped quickly around Nicholas Bos and strode toward Johnny. "Say, just who are you to butt in here? If I remember right, you're—"

"John Smith, who was a friend of Tom Quisenberry, your stepson—"

"Who murdered him!"

Johnny grinned crookedly. "No. Who was the last person to talk to Tom before he died. He told me some things, Mrs. Quisenberry. Why he ran away from his home." He turned his back upon Bonita. "Mr. Quisenberry, you were Tom's father, but just the same, before you sell the Talking Clock, I suggest you get a legal opinion. It might save you some trouble. You see, there might be other close relatives of your son, who would have a claim on the clock...."

Eric Quisenberry's eyes widened. "What are you talking about, sir?"

"Why, Tom was away from home three months before he—died. He might ... have gotten married somewhere."

"Ridiculous!"

Johnny put his tongue in his cheek. Eric stared at him for a moment, then wheeled toward his wife. Bonita Quisenberry's face had turned pale.

"Diana! . . . Do you suppose? . . ."

"I don't know," said Quisenberry hoarsely, "but even so . . ." He stared at Johnny Fletcher. "What do you know about this, sir? Speak!"

"Nothing, really. It just struck me as a possibility. After all, Tommy was practically driven from his home—"

"Driven!" Bonita Quisenberry spat, venomously. "How dare you make such a statement? Eric, order this man to leave the house."

"I was just going," Johnny said, nimbly. "I'd just like you to answer one question, Mr. Quisenberry. Did either you—or your father, Simon Quisenberry—employ a private detective named Jim Partridge?"

For a moment, Johnny thought Bonita Quisenberry would faint. She flinched as if he had struck her and her eyelids fluttered wildly.

Quisenberry, too, was affected. "Jim Partridge! Did you say, Jim *Partridge?*"

"Why, yes, a private detective. I ran into him in Columbus. He was after . . . the Talking Clock."

"It's not true," whispered Bonita Quisenberry. "I . . . I haven't heard of him in years."

Quisenberry stared at his wife, as a slow flush crept up into his face. "I think, Bonita," he said, "we must have a talk about . . . this."

"You didn't employ Partridge, then?" Johnny asked.

Quisenberry shook his head. "My father may have . . ."

When Johnny and Sam were at the door, Quisenberry called to them:

"By the way, where could I get in touch with you?"

Johnny grinned. "I'll get in touch with *you*. Goodbye, Mrs. Quisenberry."

They went through the living room to the front door and let themselves out of the house. As they walked down the hillside, Johnny said to Sam, "There's something mighty queer about this set-up...."

"Damn right there is ... the whole bunch of them is screwy. And you know why? Because they have to listen to those clocks go off every hour!"

As they passed the cottage by the gate, Johnny looked through the open door and saw the truculent gatekeeper at a telephone. Sam loitered. "Maybe he still wants to make something."

The gateman half turned from the telephone and scowled at them, but kept the receiver at his ear. Johnny and Sam went out through the gate.

In the road they looked down upon the suburban community of Hillcrest.

Sam said: "Well, do we go back to the city?"

"Yes.... After a little while."

"Ahrr! You're not going to hang around here? That Quisenberry dame is poison. She's just as apt to call the cops and have them grab us."

"Uh-uh, little Bonita will behave. That Partridge name just about floored her. I wonder who this bird Partridge is. I've a good notion to—" he grinned at Sam— "find out."

Sam groaned. "Where?"

Johnny nodded to the town of Hillcrest. "Didn't the little Rusk girl tell us she lived down there?"

"She's too young," said Sam.

"Uh-uh. They're marrying them as young as sixteen these days. Guys older than me. The Rusk kid is nineteen or twenty. Maybe she's got a sister . . . or a girl friend. For you."

Sam still scowled, but made no further protest. Walking down to the main street of the little community, Johnny went into a drugstore, leaving Sam outside. When he came out, he nodded up the street

"The Hillcrest Apartments. She lives with her mother."

Ellen Rusk answered their ring at the door of the Rusk apartment. Alarm spread quickly across her face. "You're the men who—"

"Who sold some books," Johnny said, quickly. "But don't worry about that. We're also friends of your daughter's . . . and Tom Quisenberry."

"I don't understand. Diana didn't say anything . . ."

"Didn't she tell you that two men helped her retrieve the Talking Clock in Columbus?"

"Why, yes, but you? . . ."

"Smith and Jones," said Johnny. "Your daughter isn't home?"

"I'm expecting her any minute. Why. . . . Would you come in? I guess it's all right."

"Thank you."

They entered the neatly furnished apartment. Mrs. Rusk led them to the living room and nodded to the sofa. She seated herself in an armchair.

"Mrs. Rusk," Johnny began, bluntly, "did you ever hear of a man named Jim Partridge?"

Her sudden start told them that she had. But she waited a moment before replying. "Why, yes, the present Mrs.

Quisenberry was formerly married to him."

"Oh-oh!" said Johnny. "So that's it. Did you ever meet Partridge yourself?"

"No." Ellen Rusk smiled faintly. "I imagine Jim Partridge is the skeleton in Mrs. Quisenberry's closet."

"You and Mrs. Quisenberry are friends?"

Ellen Rusk colored. "I don't see . . . just where do you come into all this, Mr.—?"

"I'm Smith. He's Jones. Why, I don't really come into it at all. Except that certain misunderstandings have arisen and Sam—I mean Jones and myself—are in considerable danger. To put it bluntly, we're fugitives from justice. Accused of . . ." He shrugged.

"Yes, I know. But . . . why do you come here, to question *me?*"

Johnny hesitated. "Your daughter was engaged to Tom Quisenberry. Although he had been gone from home for some months, your daughter, nevertheless, dashed out to Minnesota immediately upon learning that he was in trouble. She drove day and night...."

He stopped and looked sharply at Mrs. Rusk. "Were Tom Quisenberry and your daughter more than *engaged?*"

She stiffened and he saw her hands grip the arms of the chair until her knuckles were white.

"I mean," he said, softly, "had they been married . . . secretly?"

"What makes you think that?" Ellen Rusk asked in a firm, although low tone.

"Why, I made such a suggestion a little while ago to Eric Quisenberry. He was considerably wrought up about it and it struck me that *he* was more than ready to believe it."

"No," said Ellen Rusk. "My daughter was not married to Tom Quisenberry. She had, in fact—"

The door buzzer whirred and she rose quickly to her feet. "Excuse me a moment...."

She stopped. Diana Rusk came into the room. Her eyes widened when she saw Johnny and Sam. "You! . . ."

148

"Hello, Miss Rusk," Johnny said, grinning.

Ellen Rusk was making signals to her daughter, but the latter ignored them and coming forward, extended her hand to Johnny. "I got Tom's clock," she said. "And I'm glad you came here. It gives me an opportunity to thank you."

Johnny grimaced. "Why did you give the clock to Mr. Quisenberry? He came darn near selling it this afternoon."

"Why, I imagine it's his to sell now, isn't it?"

"That depends, Miss Rusk. You see, Tom's grandfather left that particular clock to Tom and—"

"Diana!" said Ellen Rusk sharply. "Please come into the bedroom with me a moment."

Johnny sighed. "A man named Bos offered seventy-five thousand dollars for the clock."

"Seventy-five thousand! . . ." gasped Diana Rusk and then her mother caught her arm and propelled her out of the room.

Johnny sat down again on the sofa. Sam said, sourly, to him: "I think we ought to get out of here, Johnny. This Mrs. Rusk is pretty upset. You've been too rough."

"I know. But it's all right. There won't be any more. I think the girl's entitled to whatever's coming to her. That Quisenberry dame would grab anything...."

Ellen and Diana Rusk came out of the bedroom. The girl's face was pale, her mother's determined. Johnny nudged Sam and got up.

"Thank you, Mrs. Rusk," he said, "but I think we must be going now. Sorry to have troubled you...."

"Don't you want the answer—to that question?"

Johnny shook his head. "No. It won't be necessary...."

"Why not? You were so insistent before."

"Sorry. I'd just come from a bout with Bon—Mrs. Quisenberry. She was pretty eager to sell the clock."

"Ah? And you think the clock should go to Diana?"

Johnny spread out his hands and looked at them. Diana Rusk said, bravely, "I *was* married to Tom. Before he went away. But . . . I don't want the clock."

Johnny nodded. "That's up to you."

"Thank you for your interest, Mr.—" Ellen Rusk looked questioningly at Johnny.

He inhaled. "John Fletcher. And this is Sam Cragg. And now, we must be going."

Out on the street, Sam Cragg said: "Now, what'd all this get you?"

"Oh," said Johnny, "information."

Sam scowled. "Look, Johnny, there's no chance to play detective around here. I know you want to. But there just ain't anything. The Kid was killed in Minnesota, fifteen hundred miles from here. That's done and there's nothing we can do about it. Why don't we just mind our own business, huh? We've got some dough and we can make some more."

"Right you are, Sam. We'll just forget the whole thing and look after ourselves.

The first thing to do is to get located. So, let's hop the old train back to the city."

13

WHEN they got off the shuttle train at Times Square and climbed up to the street, Sam Cragg said: "Where are we going to hole up?"

"Why," said Johnny, "right over there is 45th Street. Isn't there a nice, fourth-rate hotel on 45th Street?"

"Ow! The 45th Street Hotel? Peabody isn't going to welcome us."

"Nor will he turn us away. It's against the law. We've got the money to pay for a room, so . . ." They walked over to 45th Street, turned east, and after a moment went into the hotel.

The bell captain started automatically toward them, then suddenly stopped in his tracks. "Mr. Fletcher; and Sam Cragg. Holy Gee!"

"Hiyah, Eddie," Johnny greeted the bell captain. "How's things?"

"They been slow . . . until now. Uh . . . there's the boss!"

Mr. Peabody, the manager of the 45th Street Hotel, wearing his neatly pressed afternoon suit, with a white carnation in the buttonhole, descended upon them.

"Mr. Fletcher!" he exclaimed. "How *do* you do. Isn't it too bad?"

"What? Your mother-in-law coming to live with you?"

"Ha-ha," Mr. Peabody laughed, without humor. "Always joking. No, I had reference to the room situation. With the World's Fair and all—we're crowded to the roof."

"Now, *you're* kidding, Peabody. I'll bet you've got fifty rooms vacant. Why, I sent you a nice old couple this morning. Mr. and Mrs. Schultz from Iowa. Did you take good care of them?"

"Yes, yes, of course." Peabody frowned. He looked pointedly at the carton dangling from Sam's hand. "Is that your baggage?"

"For the nonce. The trunks are coming later."

Peabody pressed his lips together tightly, and shook his head. "I'm sorry, I *might* be able to find a vacant room, but since you have no baggage—"

"Tut-tut, Peabody." Johnny took a handful of crumpled bills from his pocket. "I'm holding heavy. I don't mind paying a week's rent in advance . . . since the hotel needs the money so badly. Eleven dollars, sir. There you are."

"Fifteen; our rates have gone up. . . ."

"Eleven," said Johnny firmly. "You're not going to raise *us* just because there's a World's Fair in town."

Mr. Peabody looked darkly at Johnny. "Something tells me I'm going to be sorry for this weakness."

"Mr. Peabody," said Sam Cragg, "I'd like to show you a card trick. . . ." He looked at the other's austere face and scowled. "On the other hand, let's skip it. You never did have a sense of humor."

"If I didn't," said Mr. Peabody, bitingly, "would I permit you to come back to this hotel, after what you did here last time? . . ."

Up in Room 821, Johnny took off his coat and rolling up his sleeves went into the bathroom to wash up. With the water running, he yelled to Sam:

"Look in the phone directory for the address of the Quisenberry Clock Company, and see if that Greek, Nicholas Bos, is listed in the book."

Sam Cragg came into the bathroom. "What'd you say, Johnny?"

"I said to look up the address of the Quisenberry—"

"I heard that. But Johnny, you promised you'd forget that business. Whenever you play detective, we come out the wrong end. Look what almost happened to us up there in Minnesota and we were minding our own business."

"It's because of that I'm interested in the Quisenberrys, Sam. You don't think those John Smith and John Jones alibis are going to hold forever, do you? One of these fine days someone's going to knock on our door and when we open it a man'll be standing there and he'll say: 'Mr.

Smith and Jones? The chief wants to have a word with you!'"

"But we don't have to stick here in New York now. We've got a stake and—"

"How much of a stake, Sam? I've already paid Peabody eleven bucks. Which leaves us about fifty. And what about poor Mort? You going to let that loan shark work him over?"

Sam winced. "I could beat the hell out of him, but I dunno about his gang. They don't fight with their fists...."

"Damn right they don't. We got Mort into it and we've got to get him out of it. We'll have to stick around here long enough to get him out of hock. We owe it to Mort. He's been a grand guy...."

Sam looked suspiciously at Johnny. Then he shrugged and got the phone directory. "Yeah," he said, after a moment, "the clock outfit's over on Tenth Avenue. Let's see about Bos, now. B-o-s ... mm, say, here's a Nicholas Bos with a 'b' after his name. That means business. The address is on West

Avenue.... What business would he be in? Clocks?"

"No. They're his hobby. I gathered that the Greek has plenty of what it takes. Did you hear him offer seventy-five G's for a clock?"

"I heard him and I was thinking that we practically had our mitts on that clock once. All we needed was two hundred bucks."

Johnny screwed up his mouth. "Wonder why the Kid hocked the clock for two hundred dollars when it was worth so much?"

"Maybe he didn't know how much it was worth."

Johnny shrugged and put on his coat. "It's about four thirty. We've just got time to run over to this clock outfit. I'd like to see what it looks like."

"All right," Sam sighed.

They left the hotel and walked briskly toward Seventh Avenue. They crossed Times Square and continued westward. When they reached Tenth Avenue they turned north.

Johnny whistled. "There she is! The building covers a whole block. They must have turned out a lot of Simple Simons to build that."

"Simple Simons?"

"Now, don't tell me you never saw a Simple Simon alarm clock, Sam. Every drugstore in America sells 'em. One buck per alarm."

"Oh, those! I threw one at a cat one night and when I went out the next morning there was the clock, ticking away as good as new."

They went into the building. Opposite the elevators was a receptionist behind a mahogany desk.

Johnny said: "I want to see the boss. The big boss."

"I'm sorry," the receptionist said, "but Mr. Quisenberry was buried only today."

"I know that. But the company's still in business, isn't it? Somebody must be in charge and that's who I want to see...."

"Why, yes, I think that would be Mr. Tamarack, the sales manager. But . . . do you have an appointment?"

"Does a fellow need an appointment around here to buy some clocks? Look, Miss, I'm on my vacation. I came to New York to see the World's Fair. I don't *have* to buy any clocks, but I thought as long as I was here I'd look over your line. If it's as good as the line I've been handling, well . . ."

"Of course, sir. Just a moment. . . ."

"The name is Fletcher. Of Fletcher & Company." Out of the side of his mouth he said to Sam, "You're the company."

The girl spoke into her telephone and looked up at Johnny. "Go right through this door and up the hall to Office Number Three. Mr. Tamarack will be glad to see you."

The inner hall was nicely carpeted and the walls were of pine paneling. Johnny pushed open a door bearing the gold numeral "3" and entered.

Wilbur Tamarack got up from behind a huge desk. "Mr. Fletcher? I don't believe we've ever had the pleasure of doing business with you."

He held out his hand and Johnny shook

it, nodding when Tamarack returned his grip with interest. "Glad to know you, Mr. Tamarack. This is my friend, Mr. Cragg."

"How do you do, Mr. Cragg? You're from out of town, I understand."

"That's right . . . Uh, Missouri, Kaycee."

"Kansas City? Why, I make Kansas City regularly. Where's your store, Mr. Fletcher?"

"Store? Why, I haven't got a store."

"You do a mail-order business?"

"No, of course not."

Tamarack looked startled. "But Miss Sampson said you were in the clock business!"

"What ever made her say that!" exclaimed Johnny. "I just said I wanted to buy some clocks, that was all."

"I don't understand. If you're not in the clock business . . ."

"Do I have to be in the clock business to buy a clock, Mr. Tamarack? We've always used a Simple Simon clock at home, but I took the last one apart and when I put it together there were some pieces left over. So I thought as long as I was in New York I might as well stop in here and get a new clock. My friend, Mr. Cragg, wants to buy one, too. Uh . . . do you suppose we could get anything off by buying two and because we came right here to the factory? . . .

Tamarack's face looked as if he had just come out from under an ultra-violet suntan machine. He was breathing hoarsely.

"I place you now," he said thickly. "The names didn't penetrate at first. You're the fellows who were in Minnesota with Tom Quisenberry."

"Huh!" gasped Sam Cragg.

"Minnesota?" Johnny asked softly.

Tamarack pawed the air. "Don't get excited. Diana Rusk told me about you two. How you sent her the pawn ticket in Columbus, Ohio . . . and the rest."

"Oh," said Johnny. "You know her?"

Tamarack's forehead creased. "Miss Rusk is a very good friend of mine. As for the rest—well, the sheriff of that place in Minnesota talked to me on the phone.

I passed the information on to Eric Quisenberry."

"I see. Then you know all about the case." Johnny drew a deep breath "Well, look, Mr. Tamarack, I'll lay all my cards on the table. My friend and I are in deep water. We're fugitives from Minnesota. But we didn't *have* to give that pawn ticket to Miss Rusk, in Columbus. That ought to convince you that we didn't kill Tom Quisenberry...."

"I never thought you did. Diana was convinced of your innocence. But ... if it wasn't you two, it must have been that other occupant of the jail.... There *was* another man, wasn't there?"

"There was. And he's the one who stabbed the constable and made the break. We merely lit out after him. And we didn't catch him, because he had a car waiting around the corner...."

"Diana mentioned that car. But since you were right behind him, you must have seen the license plate...."

"I did. There was a half inch of dust on it. He'd fixed that plate the night before. And I'll bet a dollar against a Simple Simon he didn't use that plate for more than two or three miles. There was something damn funny about that tramp. The Kid knew it, too. Otherwise he wouldn't have slipped me the pawn ticket during the night."

"They were in jail before you were put in?"

"Yeah. The Kid'd been in two days. The tramp was thrown in just an hour or two before we were...." Johnny cleared his throat. "Tough about the old man passing on right now."

"Simon? He's cheated the devil for the last two years."

"How come?"

Wilbur Tamarack shrugged. "He was a pretty tough old bozo. He gave no quarter and asked none. I don't think he had a friend in the world."

"Not even here in the business?"

Tamarack shook his head. "If you mean me, no. I've run this business for the last two years, since Simon took to his bed. The least I expected—" He stopped and looked shrewdly at Johnny. "How many millions would you say Simon Quisenberry left?"

"Five or ten," Johnny guessed glibly.

Tamarack smiled wickedly. "Anybody would have guessed that. Would you be surprised to know that Simon died broke? That even this business was mortgaged to the last dollar?"

Johnny blinked. "You mean he was down to his last million?"

"Last thousand. Simon was *broke*. He'd mortgaged this business for the last dollar it would bring."

"I still wouldn't call him broke. He had that little twenty-room cottage out in the country, and about half a million dollars' worth of expensive clocks...."

"All mortgaged! He borrowed a half million on the clock collection. Some Greek was stupid enough to give him the money. Well ... there's one consolation, anyway. That dope Eric will have to go to work."

"Hasn't he been working here at the plant?"

Tamarack snorted. "He's warmed a chair here, if that's what you mean. Simon didn't even trust him to lick stamps. For that matter, I doubt if he could have performed such a complicated task."

"From which I gather that you don't like Eric Quisenberry."

Tamarack scowled. "I don't. And he doesn't like me. Say . . . what are you, Fletcher? A detective?"

"Me? Gosh, no. I'm a book salesman. . . ."

"Then why the questioning?"

Johnny chuckled and stepped out.

When they left the building Sam Cragg said, "What'd this get you?"

"It got me the information that Old Simon was a hellion. And something else. Tamarack didn't go out to his funeral. And Tamarack doesn't like Eric Quisenberry either. Jealous of him."

"All right, you know that. So what good does it do you?"

"Maybe none."

They walked back to the 45th Street

Hotel and went to their room. A minute after they closed the door, there was a knock on it.

"Peabody," snorted Sam. "What the hell's he want now?"

He went to the door and opened it. Jim Partridge grinned at him. "Hello, big fellow."

Sam Cragg made noises in his throat. Johnny looking over Sam's shoulder, said: "Come in, Partridge. Just the man we've been looking for."

Partridge came in and closed the door. "I'll bet you've been looking for me."

"Why, sure. I didn't want to scare you away on the street, so I let you follow us here."

"Huh?"

Johnny grunted. "You were hanging around outside the Quisenberry Clock Company. You saw us come out and followed us here."

"You're guessing. You didn't see me."

"All right, we didn't. But it had to be that way, because no one knew we'd checked into this hotel. So—what's on your mind, Partridge?"

Partridge rubbed his jaw. "You didn't think I'd stay in Columbus, did you?"

Sam Cragg growled. He suddenly pinned Partridge's arms to his sides. Then releasing one hand he frisked the private detective. The result was an automatic which he tossed to one of the beds.

"If you'd asked me nice I'd have put it there myself," Partridge said.

"Sure, you would," said Cragg. "But I'm feeling mean today and I didn't want to have to break your jaw first."

"You're pretty tough," Partridge commented, reflectively.

"Tough enough."

"Sit down, Partridge," said Johnny. "We'll have a talk. I know more now than I did in Columbus. . . . I've seen your ex-wife."

"Bonita? How is she?"

"Don't you know?"

"Haven't seen her in five years."

"You're not working with her?"

Partridge chuckled. "I'm working for myself."

"Nuts!"

"Believe it or not, Fletcher. Talk to Bonita sometime. Bet she'll tell you she'd rather see a lot of people than me. I know where the body is buried."

"Where?"

"That's one of my hole cards. Look, Fletcher, I underestimated you in Ohio. But you pulled a fool stunt by turning over that clock to the Rusk kid. That thing was worth a lot of dough."

"That's right. But I did turn it over to the girl. So?..."

"Simon Quisenberry was worth a lot of money."

"Guess again. He died broke. All he left was this clock."

"Nah," said Partridge. "He had a clock collection worth a million bucks. And a big estate, not to mention the Simple Simon Clock outfit, which isn't hay in itself."

"Everything mortgaged. Even the

clocks. Except the one—the Talking Clock. He left that to his grandson."

"Who died before Simon did."

Johnny looked thoughtfully at the private detective. "How does that figure out? Did the clock revert back to the estate?"

"Depends on the wording of Old Simon's will. In either case, the clock is worth plenty by itself. I figure the clock can be had."

"Through your hole card, Bonita?"

Partridge frowned. "You don't know the old girl. I was married to her. Do you see that brass ash stand there? It's soft stuff compared to Bonita. She's out for herself, first, last and all the time."

"I gathered that. Her present husband, Eric, has about as much chance as a mouse would have in a college of cats. But for the time being, I think Bonita is stymied. Nothing she can do . . . except leave her husband."

"She'll leave him when she's got his last dollar. Not before. Bonita's tough,

Fletcher, but would you believe that I had her housebroken?"

"Meaning that you're a tough bozo yourself?"

Partridge smiled modestly. "Remember the Monahan-Royster case four years ago? I pinched Monahan."

"All right," agreed Johnny. "You're tough. So what?"

"So I thought we might play ball. What were you doing over at the Quisenberry Clock Company?"

"I was trying to buy a Simple Simon Clock."

Partridge's eyes glittered. "What's your interest in this, Fletcher? You had the clock once and gave it to the girl. Why do you stick around then?"

"Why?" said Johnny. "A kid I was in jail with got himself murdered and the Minnesota cops seem to think me and Sam here did it. I'm trying to prove we didn't."

"That was Minnesota; this is New York."

"They can extradite you for a murder rap."

"Yeah," said Jim Partridge, thoughtfully. "So they can."

"Don't go getting ideas, Partridge," growled Sam Cragg.

"By the way," said Johnny, "could you prove where *you* were on September 19th?"

"I wasn't in Minnesota."

"Can you prove you weren't?"

"Can you prove I was?"

"No," said Johnny, "but Sam and me could swear that the guy who was in jail with us—the one who struck the constable—looked a lot like you, without your face washed. Catch on?"

"Don't worry. I'm not going to snitch to the cops about you. I've got a stake in this game and I'll play my cards without cops. But I'm warning you. I play a tough game."

"Swell," said Sam Cragg. "So do we. And as long as warnings are in order, let me give you one, Partridge. Next time you see us coming, cross the street."

Partridge smiled icily. "Can I take my hardware with me? It isn't loaded, anyway."

Johnny picked up the automatic from the bed and saw that the magazine was empty. He tossed the gun to Partridge.

"So long, Partridge."

"Just for a while. I may see you around." He looked pointedly at Sam Cragg. "Both of you."

After he had gone out, Sam Cragg shivered. "Something tells me that Partridge is a mean hombre."

"I remember him now. Monahan was a killer and he had some rough boys with him. Partridge went into his hide-out and killed one of the hoods and beat the hell out of this Monahan."

"And did you hear what he said about his ex?"

"About having had her housebroken? Did you see her face this morning? She was scared stiff when I mentioned his name. I thought at the time it was because I'd spilled something. I guess maybe it was because she's afraid of Partridge. Well, how about some food now, Sam?"

"I'm ready. I still haven't got over those lean days. A nice, thick steak, smothered in onions . . . and maybe a few pork chops for dessert. . . ."

14

JOHNNY was lying in bed the next morning, wondering whether to get up and dress or have breakfast brought up to the room. He rolled his head and saw the newspaper under the door, and after looking at it a while, decided that he might as well get up and see what was going on.

He got the newspaper and returned to bed. In the twin bed on the side nearest the windows Sam Cragg was lying on his back, covers thrown back. He wore no pajamas and his broad chest was rising and falling rhythmically.

Johnny looked at the newspaper. The British were giving the Germans hell and the Germans were beating the hell out of the British. The British downed fourteen German planes, with a loss of but one for their side and the Germans had shot down thirty-four British planes with a loss of only two of their own.

Then an item on the bottom half of the front page caught his eye:

FAMOUS TALKING CLOCK STOLEN

QUISENBERRY MANSION IN HILLCREST BURGLARIZED

According to the account, Joe Cornish, manager of the Quisenberry estate, had surprised a pair of burglars on the Quisenberry estate shortly after midnight. He had fought with the men, but they had overpowered him and made their escape. Reporting the occurrence to the owner of the estate, Eric Quisenberry, an examination was made in the house with the astonishing discovery that the safe was open and the famous Talking Clock, valued at $100,000 by the recently deceased owner, Simon Quisenberry, was missing. The burglars had not touched any of the other clocks in the famous collection, most of which were not under lock and key.

Johnny rolled up the newspaper and reaching over, slapped Sam Cragg's bare chest. "Up, Sammy, my boy! The sun's shining and the early birds are getting all the worms. . . . We've been outwitted."

Sam Cragg sat up and blinked stupidly. "Owoo!" he yawned. "What's matter? I was just dreaming that we were in Florida and I'd picked a thirty-two to one shot—"

"And the horse stumbled in the stretch! Look at this paper, Sam. The Talking Clock's been swiped from the Quisenberrys."

"Huh? Say. . . . Jim Partridge?"

"Read the description that bird Cornish gave of the burglars. One man tall and rather slender, the other shorter and very stocky. An extraordinarily powerful man. . . ."

"Hey! Those're our descriptions."

"Were we at the Quisenberry estate around midnight?"

"We were pounding our ears here."

"Sure we were. So let's get out there and tell them."

Sam winced. "Is that a good idea? This Cornish lad may identify us. He didn't seem to care a lot for either of us."

"I didn't care for him, either. But he won't identify us. He didn't mention having actually recognized the burglars, did he? Furthermore . . . there's something damn fishy about this burglary. Why should they pass up the other clocks? If you'll remember, some of them looked even better than the Talking Clock."

"But they weren't worth as much."

"Only a clock expert would know that. Or someone who knew about the Talking Clock."

Johnny hopped out of bed and headed for the bathroom. When he came out a few minutes later, he began dressing. "Hurry up, Sam," he said. "We've got a busy day ahead of us. . . ."

It was then that the door resounded to the rapping of knuckles. Johnny slipped on his trousers and began buttoning his shirt. Still shoeless, he went to the door.

"Who is it?"

"Me," said the voice of Jim Partridge.

"Ah, hell! Before breakfast." However, Johnny opened the door. He regretted it instantly.

Partridge had a friend with him, a man who outweighed Sam Cragg by twenty pounds and most certainly had been either a prizefighter or wrestler at some time. He couldn't have acquired such a battered face and such thick ears in ordinary encounters.

Sam began growling.

"Easy, boys," said Jim Partridge. "I'm not looking for trouble. Not now. This is one of my operators. Call him Hutch."

"The name is Hutchinson," said Hutch. "Edgar Hutchinson. But don't call me Edgar."

"Shut up, Edgar," Partridge said. "Look, Fletcher, I see you've got a paper. You've read about the clock."

"Just finished. Why'd you do it, Partridge?"

"The watchman's description fits you birds."

"We were sleeping at midnight."

"That's what the bell captain says. I asked him before we came up. But you might have slipped him something. He seemed to be on your side, all the way."

"Eddie Miller? Yep, he practically works for me. So does Peabody, the manager. Get to the point, Partridge."

"I am. You didn't steal the clock and I didn't. Who did?"

"Maybe it was an inside job. Your ex. . . ."

Partridge glowered. "She's not beyond it, but the watchman described these two pugs—"

"Maybe the watchman's a friend of Bonita's." Johnny did not know how accurate was his guess.

"What's he look like?"

"Don't you know?"

Partridge grunted. "How should I? I've never been out there."

"In Columbus you said you were representing the Quisenberry estate."

"That was in Columbus. I'm working for myself, Fletcher."

"Well, you want to watch yourself. You might forget and cut your own throat."

Sam Cragg snickered and Partridge scowled. "Cut the comedy, Fletcher. I'm not ready to go out to the Quisenberry place yet. How's about you running out there and finding out what's what?"

"Uh-uh, Partridge. You look like a monkey all right, but we're out of chestnuts today. I'm working for myself, too."

"I've been thinking it over," Partridge said, deliberately, "I've got an alibi for September 29th. . . ."

Johnny looked pointedly at Hutch. "What was your ring name, Stupid?"

"Stupid?" yelped Hutch. "Why you—"

Sam Cragg took one step forward and hit Hutch on the side of the head with his fist. Hutch reeled to the wall, hit and ricocheted back. Sam clipped him on the chin, scarcely seeming to exert himself. Hutch fell to the floor on his face.

While this was going on, Johnny Fletcher stepped close to Jim Partridge, so he could block any move Partridge might make. Partridge watched what happened to his operator, his nostrils flaring. When Hutch hit the floor he said: "I guess I'll have to fire him. He told me he could take it."

"How about you, Partridge?" Sam invited. "You look pretty husky yourself. . . ."

"I'll wait till I've got some brass knuckles with me."

Johnny gestured to Sam and the big fellow walked around behind Partridge and pinned his arms to his sides. Johnny relieved Partridge of his automatic. He scowled. "You've got some bullets today, I see."

He slipped out the magazine and tossed it into the wastebasket. Then he proceeded to frisk Partridge further. He returned everything to the private detective's pockets, except a crumpled telegram.

"Listen to this, Sam!" he exclaimed.

"'James Partridge, Sorenson Hotel, New York. Collect Answer your wire. Not interested Smith and Jones. Inquest determined Quisenberry suicide. Fitch wound mere scratch. Besides this country has no money to send officer to New York, Doolittle, Sheriff Brooklands County, Minnesota.'"

"Why the rat!" snarled Sam Cragg.

"I thought there was something fishy about his threat. He didn't have time to get himself an out-of-town alibi since last night and he wouldn't have dared call us without a good alibi."

"Shall I let him have it, Johnny?"

"You're one up on me already," Partridge replied. "Better not make it two."

"I don't get this telegram, Johnny," said Sam. "How could a guy commit suicide by choking himself?"

"He didn't. He was murdered all right. This hick county just doesn't want to spend any money extraditing anyone and then prosecuting him. They're taking the cheapest way out by calling it suicide."

"Where's the truck that hit me?" mumbled Hutch, sitting up.

Partridge kicked him in the ribs. "On your feet, Stumblebum!"

Knuckles massaged the door of Room 821 and Mr. Peabody's voice called. "Mr. Fletcher, what are you doing in there? The guests are complaining about the racket you're creating."

Johnny opened the door. "Ah, good morning, Mr. Peabody. We were just doing our daily calisthenics. . . ."

Peabody looked at Hutch who was climbing unsteadily to his feet.

"Our physical culture instructor," Johnny said. "He comes every morning to give us a workout. See you tomorrow, eh, Professor?"

Jim Partridge grabbed Hutch's arm and propelled him past Peabody, into the corridor. Peabody still glowered at Johnny.

"I knew I was making a mistake, Mr.

Fletcher. You're mixed up in something again. . . ."

"Why, Mr. Peabody," Johnny said, reproachfully. "I'm beginning to think you don't appreciate guests who pay in advance, by the week . . ."

"Ah!" cried Peabody, throwing his hands into the air and turning away.

Sam Cragg kicked the door shut. It made a good loud slam. "Well, that settles that, Johnny. Since Minnesota no longer wants us, we can drop out of the Quisenberry business."

"Why," said Johnny, "if the law's no longer interested in punishing a culprit, it's up to the private citizen and you and I, Sam—"

Sam put his head between his hands and groaned. "Trouble, here we come again!"

They left the hotel ten minutes later and had breakfast at the orange stand on the corner, a glass of orange juice, two doughnuts and a cup of coffee. Finished, Johnny hailed a taxicab.

Sam grumbled as they got in. "A ten-cent breakfast and then a taxi. . . ."

"We're in a hurry. West Avenue, Cabby."

"The clock man, huh?"

"That's right. I want to see whether he looks happy or mad today. He was pretty keen about that clock yesterday."

Twenty minutes later they climbed out of the taxi before a tall building, facing the Hudson River docks. Johnny paid the taxi bill, adding a nickel tip, over which the cabby muttered, then faced the building.

"Aegean Sponge Company," he read the inscription on the brass plate beside the door of the building. "Nicholas Bos, President. You wouldn't think they sold enough sponges in this country for that bird to pay seventy-five G's for a fancy clock."

They went into the building. A receptionist with buck teeth and a complexion like Roquefort cheese had them spell out their names, then telephoned them to an unknown person. After a moment she covered the mouthpiece. "What is your business?"

"Clocks," said Johnny. "We met Mr. Bos in Hillcrest yesterday."

The girl relayed the additional information, then nodded. The door beside her desk burst open and the olive-skinned Nicholas Bos reached out with both hands.

"Come in, gentlemen. I am so glad seeing you. Come in, please!"

They followed the sponge importer to an office which contained forty or fifty clocks, all of them showing the correct time, nine forty-eight.

Bos closed the door and turned eagerly to them. "Yes, gentlemen? You have gome to sell . . ."

"Sell what, Mr. Bos?"

"The clock maybe?"

"The Talking Clock?"

Nicholas Bos almost drooled. "You have it? . . ." he whispered.

"No," said Johnny. "It was stolen last night from the Quisenberry house."

Disappointment swept across the

importer's olive face. "But I am reading that in the paper. I t'ink maybe you . . ."

"Why should you think we stole it?"

"But you are what you call—ex-gonvic'. I am seeing you yesterday and this morning when I am reading in the paper, I t'ink, they have stolen the clock, those gonvic's...."

"I figured *you* for the burglar," Johnny said bluntly.

"And I'm not an ex-convict," Sam added.

"Oh! I am so sorry. But Meesus Queesenberry, she say . . ."

"Since I'm a gentleman," said Johnny, "I can't say anything against a lady. Except that Mrs. Quisenberry reminds me of a clip-joint taxi dancer who picked my pocket one time."

"Ah, then you don't having the clock?"

"That's the general idea, Mr. Bos. I came here to get some information about that clock. What makes it worth so much money?"

"Because is Talking Clock."

"I could have a small phonograph made

and put in a Simple Simon clock for a hundred bucks. It would talk and it wouldn't be worth a lot of money."

"Ah, but this clock is very, very old. Three hundred year. Four hundred—"

"Going at five," chimed in Sam Cragg.

"Five? No. Not that old. Is beautiful work. Fine engraving and the jewel . . . worth much money alone."

"Melted down, how much would it bring?"

"Melted down?" Horror popped wide Bos' eyes. "You would not melt down this beautiful clock, Mister. Oh no. Don't doing that! . . ."

"I'm not melting it down. I haven't got the clock. I'm just trying to get an idea how much the thing'd be worth as old gold. . . ."

"Old gold? Oh, not much. The jewels, yes, are worth maybe five t'ousand dollar. But I giving fifty t'ousand—"

"You said seventy-five yesterday."

"That's right. I give you seventy-five t'ousand dollar for the clock."

"You ought to hire a detective to locate it, Mr. Bos."

"A detective? A policeman? . . ."

"No, a private detective. There's a lot of them, you know. They work for you, not the city. You could get an awfully good man . . . for about a hundred bucks a day, with a small bonus when he finishes. . . ."

"You know good detective?"

Johnny spread out his hands and looked at them, modestly. "I've had some good results as a detective. You know, I returned the clock to Diana Rusk, after locating it in Ohio. . . ."

"Yes, I am hearing. Ha! I do it. I hiring you find the Talking Clock. You bring him to me and I give you beeg bonus . . . Maybe ten t'ousand dollar."

"And the hundred dollars a day."

Bos frowned a moment, then beamed. "Fine, I also paying that. How many day you t'ink it take?"

"Not more than five or six . . . if I'm lucky."

"Is fine. I am hiring you."

"How about a couple of days' pay in advance? It's customary. Sort of retainer, you know. . . ."

The sponge importer took a long, flat wallet from his inside breast pocket and skinned out two bills. Each was a hundred-dollar denomination.

He showed even, white teeth in a wide smile. "You are sport, Mister Fletcher? Tossing coin, double or nothing?"

"Nix, Johnny," Sam Cragg said out of the side of his mouth.

Bos took a half dollar from his pocket. "You call? . . ."

"Tails," said Johnny.

Bos flipped the coin into the air, caught it and smacked it on the back of his left hand. He uncovered it. "Heads, sorry. . . ."

Sam groaned. "Looks like I've got to save the day, now . . ." He drew out his pack of cards from his pocket. "How much change we got, Johnny? We'll cut Mr. Bos high card for it. Huh? . . ." He half turned his face and winked at Johnny.

Johnny looked thoughtfully at Sam for a moment, then he drew out all the money they had in the world. He counted out fifty dollars and put two dollars and some silver back into his pocket.

"We'll cut you high card for fifty dollars, Mr. Bos."

"Why not?"

Sam riffled the cards, squared them and slapped the deck on the importer's desk.

Bos placed his hand over the cards, pressed down on them and cut. He held up the ace of spades.

Sam exclaimed in horror and a shudder seemed to run through his body.

"Go ahead and cut," Johnny said coldly. "Maybe you can get an ace yourself and tie."

"Sure," said Nicholas Bos, cheerfully.

Sam's trembling hand fumbled with the remaining cards. Finally he picked up part of them and revealed the three of diamonds.

"You win," he said, thickly.

"Some fun, yes?" Bos smiled fondly.

"You coming my apartment some time and playing poker. I like gamble."

"So do we," said Johnny, glaring at Sam Cragg.

When they reached the street, Johnny caught Sam's arm in a savage grip. "You sap! What'd you have to pull out those cards for?"

"Because they're stripped, Johnny!" gasped Sam. "I—I fixed them, so I could cut the ace myself and he beat me to it."

"Why, the dirty—!" Johnny swore. "He outslicked us all around. I didn't like that coin toss of his."

"Neither did I. I was reading in my book about tossing coins and there're six or seven ways you can beat a man. That's —that's why I tried the card cutting."

Johnny pulled out the remainder of their stake and gave Sam one of the crumpled bills. "Not enough for us both to run out to Hillcrest. You'll have to stay in town. Here's some money for grub. Go easy."

Sam was too crestfallen to protest over Johnny's going out to Hillcrest. He merely asked, weakly: "When'll you be back?"

"When you see me," Johnny snapped. "You might run over to Mort's and get some more books—"

"Ouch!" cried Sam. "We promised to bring him some money today."

"You lost the money. You and your card tricks. Tell that to Mort. And you might show him the rest of your tricks. Carmella, too, if he comes around while you're there. . . . So long, Sam. . . ."

Johnny headed for the subway toward which they had been walking.

15

WHEN Johnny got to the Grand Central Terminal he discovered that the Hillcrest train had just left and that the next did not go for an hour and twenty minutes. Annoyed, he went to the battery of telephone booths and looked in the classified phone directory. After a moment, he nodded in satisfaction and left the station.

On Lexington Avenue he caught a north-bound bus and rode to 60th Street. He swung off there and walked back a little way to a shop that had a depressed window, completely filled with clocks. He stepped down the few stairs to the door of the shop and pushed it open.

The ticking of a hundred clocks hit his ears. An elderly man with a white goatee and a black skull cap greeted him from behind a long counter filled with clocks.

"Mr. McAdam?" Johnny said. "I'm

from the *Daily Blade*. I'm doing a story on clocks and I've heard that you're the foremost authority on them in New York. I thought perhaps you might give me a bit of information...."

"On clocks, sir? of course. I presume Quisenberry's Talking Clock prompted this sudden clock interest, Mr.—?"

"Fletcher. And you're quite right, Mr. McAdam. My city editor suggested the clock story. He didn't seem to believe that the Quisenberry clock was as valuable as the family claimed."

McAdam shrugged. "A clock is worth whatever the seller can get. Just like a stamp or a rare coin. I've seen Quisenberry's clock. It is undoubtedly an authentic example of early sixteenth century workmanship. According to the history of the clock, it was made in Seville for Queen Isabella...."

"Queen Isabella? Say, that's interesting. The clock's four hundred years old then?"

"A little more. It was supposed to have

been made in 1506. The main part of the clock, of course."

"It's been rebuilt?"

McAdam smiled. "After all, Thomas Edison didn't invent the talking machine until forty-some years ago."

Johnny was chagrined. "I never thought of that. But I've seen the clock, Mr. Mc—"

"When? It's disappeared...."

"Yes of course. Uh... I saw the clock several months ago. I was sent out to interview Simon Quisenberry on some other matter. He had the clock set up in his room. It struck the hour and a door opened and the little man came out and said his piece."

"The mannikin is from the original clock. That hasn't been changed. Originally, chimes played 'Ave Maria.' I thought myself the clock should never have been changed, but Simon was always one to indulge a whim and he had the talking box put in in place of the chimes. Phonographs were still a novelty then and the clock always attracted a good deal of attention when he exhibited it."

"I didn't know he exhibited it."

McAdam tugged gently at his goatee. "A collector who wouldn't exhibit his collection? There's no such animal, Mr. Fletcher."

"I guess you're right. Well, then, Mr. McAdam, you think the clock's really worth a hundred thousand dollars?"

"A hundred thousand! . . . What are you talking about?"

"Why, I understand that Nicholas Bos has already offered the family seventy-five thousand for it and they're holding out for a hundred. . . ."

"That's preposterous! Five thousand would be a good price for it. Surely no more than ten."

"But I heard Bos—I mean, I got it on good authority that Bos actually made that offer for it."

"A publicity offer, Mr. Fletcher. Don't believe it. Sounds like Bos. He's always been a four-flusher. He may pay a little more than a clock's worth if he can get some free advertising out of it, but he certainly wouldn't pay any such price as you mention. He drives a good bargain. I've sold him some pieces myself."

"Well," said Johnny. "That puts a new light on things. Now, tell me, Simon's collection is pretty good, isn't it? How much would you estimate it to be worth?"

"Why, if it includes the Empress Catherine's famous egg clock, a half million would be cheap."

"Wait a minute, now! What's this Empress Catherine egg clock?"

"It's a watch, really. It contains a ruby that's worth a hundred thousand alone."

"Ah," said Johnny. "But the Talking Clock also contains jewels...."

"Some small carat stuff. If you remember your history, you know that Queen Isabella wasn't wealthy. She had to pawn some of her jewels to pay for Columbus' expedition. I still think ten thousand would be a good price for the Talking Clock. The Empress Catherine's egg clock is something else. But its value lies in the ruby, not the clock."

Johnny looked at one of the clocks behind McAdam. "Thanks a lot, Mr. McAdam. I've got to run now."

"No hurry, Mr. Fletcher. I'm not busy and I'd like to give you some more data on clocks...."

"Sorry, but I've got to meet a deadline."

"Oh, I see. Well, come around again. When will your article be in the paper? This afternoon?"

"Uh—no! This is a feature story for our Sunday supplement. Thanks a lot, Mr. McAdam."

Johnny ran out of the store and fortunately caught a bus on the corner going back to the Grand Central. He made the Hillcrest train with two minutes to spare.

Walking through the business street of Hillcrest, on his way to the Rusk apartment, Johnny Fletcher spied Diana Rusk on the other side of the street. He crossed over to meet her.

"Morning, Miss Rusk. I was just on my way to see you."

"Mr. Fletcher! I've been wondering

how to get in touch with you. I suppose you've heard about—the clock?"

"That's why I came out here. May I walk with you?"

"I'm on my way to Twelve O'Clock House."

"Twelve O'Clock House? That's the Quisenberry place? Swell, I'll walk with you. I was going to go there later on. . . . What do you think of this theft? The paper said the watchman—"

"Cornish would be insulted to hear you call him a watchman. He's the estate manager. Yes, I heard his description of the—the marauders."

"I was sleeping at the 45th Street Hotel at the time. I can prove it. But tell me about this Cornish fellow. How long has he worked on the estate?"

"Two or three years. He . . ." Diana made a wry face. "This sounds catty, but Bonita—I mean, Mrs. Quisenberry, is rather, shall we say, fond of Joe Cornish?"

"Oh—oh! I made a guess like that just

yesterday. By the way, that was for Jim Partridge's benefit."

"Partridge! Is he here?"

"And how! He brought one of his gorillas to the hotel the first thing this morning. Sam slapped down the gorilla."

"I don't understand his interest in this. Unless Bonita . . ."

"He says no. And yesterday when I mentioned his name in front of Bonita she almost threw in the sponge. She seemed scared just at the mention of Partridge's name."

Diana's smooth forehead creased. She shot a sidewise glance at Johnny, then looked straight ahead.

"Mr. Quisenberry came down to see us after you'd gone yesterday. He—he asked about my marriage to Tom."

"Did you tell him?"

"I saw no reason to keep it a secret . . . now."

"What'd he say?"

"Why . . . he was very nice about it. It—it wasn't Mr. Quisenberry who objected. . . ."

"Ah, the gentle Bonita. People might think she was getting along if a daughter-in-law suddenly showed up."

"How old do you think Bonita is?"

Johnny pursed his lips. "Oh, about thirty. Well, maybe thirty-two or three."

Diana sniffed scornfully. "That shows how much a man knows about a woman. Bonita's type. She's as old as my mother."

"Huh? She—doesn't look it."

"She tries hard enough not to. I—I don't like her. If it hadn't been for her, Tom wouldn't be—"

Johnny changed the subject quickly. "By the way, have you ever met this clock collector, Nicholas Bos?"

She flashed him a smile. "Once or twice. He came to see old Mr. Quisenberry now and then."

They had climbed the steep hill to the gate of Twelve O'Clock House by this time and Johnny was caught again by the queer diagonal macadam paths leading away from the house.

"Say," he exclaimed, "those paths are fixed up like the dial of a clock."

"Of course," said Diana. "That's why the house is called Twelve O'Clock House. There are twelve such paths . . . the drive here is six o'clock, the walk to the right, five o'clock and so on—Shh!"

Joe Cornish came out of his cottage, a piece of adhesive tape stuck over his right cheekbone.

"Good morning, Joe," said Diana. "I believe Mr. Quisenberry is expecting me."

"'Morning, Miss Rusk." Cornish opened the gate, but looked sullenly at Johnny Fletcher.

"Hi, Cornish," Johnny said, flippantly. "Hear you had a little brush with burglars last night."

Cornish's mouth twisted. "Yeah. . . . I almost got them, too. One of them looked like . . ." He shrugged.

Johnny winked and walked past the surly estate manager. As they climbed up the walk, Eric Quisenberry got up from a wicker chair on the veranda and came to meet them.

"Good morning, Diana." He squinted at Johnny. "And Mr. Fletcher."

"Did I get here too early?" Diana asked.

"No. Mr. Walsh is already here. He's in the house with my—with Bonita. Uh, Mr. Fletcher, would you mind waiting out here a few minutes? It's—Mr. Walsh was my father's attorney and . . ."

"Of course. I'll sit down right here."

Eric Quisenberry took Diana Rusk into the house and Johnny seated himself in the wicker chair. From his position he could look down over the sloping lawns and drives to the Hillcrest road, running along the front of the property.

The macadam walks that divided the estate into pie-shaped wedges fascinated Johnny. Six o'clock was the drive leading up to the house. Johnny could also see the four, five and the seven and eight o'clock walks.

Johnny wondered if old Simon Quisenberry hadn't been touched on the subject of clocks. He had put the Simple Simon clock into half the households of the United States and many foreign countries. Not content with that he had taken to collecting a half million dollars' worth of antique clocks and finally carried the clock theme into his very dwelling place.

Well, he had died. But by his clocks he would be remembered.

After a while Johnny heard voices in the house and then footsteps. The Quisenberrys, Diana Rusk and a tall, gray-haired man came out.

Bonita Quisenberry ignored Johnny, but her husband introduced the gray-haired man. "Mr. Walsh, Mr. Fletcher.... Well, good-bye, Mr. Walsh, thank you for your kindness."

The Quisenberry lawyer went off down the drive. Johnny, watching, saw Bonita's eyes smoldering as she regarded the retreating figure.

"Everything fine, Mr. Quisenberry?" Johnny said, casually.

Eric Quisenberry gave a start. "Fine? Uh, yes, yes. I mean, no. Father stated in the will that he'd made an outright gift of the clock to my son, Tom. Walsh construed that to mean that the clock belonged to Tom before Father died."

"Which is just too bad," Bonita said, nastily, "since the clock has been stolen."

Diana Rusk's chin came up proudly. "I wouldn't have accepted it, anyway."

"No? Well, I'm not accusing you, but you cultivate strange friends. Convicts—"

"Bonita!" Eric Quisenberry said, sharply.

"You!. . ." Bonita said witheringly to her husband, then turned and stormed into the house.

"I'm sorry," Quisenberry apologized. "Bonita's a bit upset."

"'S all right. I was just going," said Johnny. He stepped off the veranda, then hesitated. "I wonder if you'd mind telling me something, Mr. Quisenberry. You know I have an interest in the Talking Clock. Was the clock really in the safe last night? . . ."

"Of course. Since I knew its value, I wouldn't have left it out."

"That's what I thought. But some of those other clocks are valuable too, and they're not in the safe."

Quisenberry frowned. "To tell you the truth, I haven't been very interested in the other clocks. While Father was alive he practically lived in the room with the clocks and of course we have a watchman on the grounds, full time. . . ."

"He wasn't much good last night."

"I know," Quisenberry said, testily. "He hasn't been much good for anything lately. As a matter of fact, I'm thinking of discharging him."

Johnny nodded and was about to carry the conversation along, when Diana Rusk said, somewhat hastily, "I must be going home."

Quisenberry was already going into the house, so Johnny shrugged and fell in beside Diana. As they walked down toward the gate, he said:

"I was going to ask him something else, but I guess he was too sore. Uh . . . it's about a rumor I heard in town. Although I don't suppose there's anything to it."

"You mean," said Diana, "about Mr. Simon Quisenberry's will?"

"Yes. The story is that he didn't leave quite as much money as—well, as expected."

"That's true, Mr. Fletcher. I don't suppose it'll remain a secret very long. Actually, Mr. Simon left nothing at all."

"Nothing? You mean, comparatively nothing?"

"No, I mean it literally. Mr. Simon had had business reverses and I understand that he mortgaged everything he owned. Even his clock collection. . . ."

"The clock collection? Who'd loan money on that?"

"Why, that Greek sponge importer, Mr. Nicholas Bos."

Johnny blinked. "You mean all those clocks go to him? I heard him say yesterday he'd come for the clocks, but I hadn't dreamed he was referring to Simon's entire collection. Why, it's worth half million dollars, I understand."

"That's right, Mr. Quisenberry borrowed a half million dollars on it."

Johnny whistled. "And Bos is willing to go another seventy-five thousand for the Talking Clock?"

"So I understand."

Johnny shook his head. "Some people are screwy. Take yourself, why should you kick seventy-five thousand dollars in the face?"

"I think that should be obvious. When I married Tom I did so because—because I loved him. I didn't marry him for his money, like . . ."

"Like Bonita married Tom's father? Yeah, I think I begin to understand. Which reminds me, what becomes of Eric? The old man left him the business? . . ."

"What there is of it. Mother—I mean, I understand he's getting only six months with it. If he is unable to pay back the million dollars the company owes the bank, they will take everything from him."

"Oh—oh! Not so good. Tell me, this

fellow who's running the business now—Wilbur Tamarack—where does he come in?"

Her mouth seemed to tighten a little. "Why . . . why, I guess he may lose his position. You see . . . I might as well tell you. Eric never did much in the firm. Simon ran everything himself . . . with the help of Mr. Tamarack. He . . . he didn't think Eric very capable and so . . ."

"I see. But now Eric's in charge. For six months, at least. He may resent Tamarack's former authority and kick him out."

They were approaching the bridge which ran over the train tracks, beyond which was Hillcrest's mainstreet.

"I get my train back to the city here," Johnny said. "I'd like to ask you just one more question. . . . What does your mother think of Eric Quisenberry?"

He looked at the girl's widened eyes and said, quickly: "Never mind answering that." She didn't have to answer; her face told him.

He watched her walk up the street toward the Hillcrest Apartments, then finally turned to the railroad station.

16

BACK in the city, Johnny discovered, as he walked from the Grand Central to the 45th Street Hotel, that his entire capital consisted of thirty-two cents. He wondered how much of the dollar he had given Sam the latter had spent for lunch. There ought to be enough left for a moderate dinner.

He entered the hotel and the bell captain advanced toward him. "Sam's in the cocktail lounge, Mr. Fletcher." He winked. "He's picked himself up a pip."

"Sam—a pip?" Johnny was startled. But not more so than a moment later when he entered the cocktail lounge and saw the blonde who sat across a table from Sam.

The bell captain had not overstated. The girl was a knockout. Blonde, with a figure. Her complexion was entirely due to excellent make-up, but it was a fine job.

Sam was positively drooling as he regarded his conquest. But when Johnny approached and Sam looked up, he flinched and turned a deep crimson.

"Johnny!"

"Hello, Sam," Johnny said, coldly. "How's everything?"

"Uh . . . uh, fine, Johnny. Uh, meet Miss Dalton."

The girl turned mascaraed orbs upon Johnny. "And so you're Johnny Fletcher! Sam's been raving about you for two hours. Mmm . . . the name's Vivian, to you."

Johnny sat down on the cushioned bench beside Sam Cragg.

"Where'd you pick him up?" he asked Vivian, bluntly.

"Pick him up? Why . . . he insisted on buying a drink for me. But . . . are you his keeper?"

"Yes." He poked his elbow in Sam's ribs. "Since you're buying drinks, how about ordering one for me?"

"Uh, sure," grunted Sam. He signaled to the bartender. "What'll you have, Johnny?"

"Since you're drinking martinis, I'll have one, too."

"Sure, three martinis, bartender." Out of the corner of his mouth, Sam whispered, "He's a new man, here."

Johnny winced. "So you're learning, Sam . . . Well, what have you been doing all morning? Did you see Mort?"

"Oh, sure. He's . . . coming to see us some time today."

"What for?"

"You know what for." Sam chuckled. "Like to see a new trick?"

"No."

Sam picked up a package of cigarettes from the table, lit one and puffed on it. After a moment, he pulled out his handkerchief and flipped it out. "Watch now."

He spread the handkerchief in his left hand, took the cigarette in his right and stuffed it into the handkerchief, about which he closed his fist.

"Isn't he clever?" Vivian Dalton exclaimed.

Sam opened his hands, flipped the handkerchief and showed that the cigarette had disappeared—without burning the handkerchief.

"Not bad, huh, Johnny?"

"It'd be a better trick with a clean handkerchief."

Sam grimaced. "The darn laundry. But look, here's another trick." He took a cigarette holder from his pocket, stuffed a cigarette into it and lit it. He puffed, "Watch now."

There was a faint click and the cigarette disappeared from the holder.

"Gadgets," grunted Johnny.

"I was over at Max Holden's Magic Shop. There was a magician there. Look. . . ." Sam took a brand-new pack of cards from his pocket, squared them and gripped the deck in his left hand. He let half of them fall back into his palm and attempted a one-hand cut. He only attempted it, for the cards spilled from his hand to the table.

Johnny chuckled and his annoyance at his friend disappeared.

Vivian Dalton sensed it and leaned across the table. "I just checked in here today. Glad there are some interesting people. I'm in the show at the Lucky Seven Club. Why don't you and Sam run over tonight and see me do my stuff?"

"With a bottle of beer selling at seventy-five cents, Sam and I could buy about a thimbleful and I'm afraid they don't sell beer in such small quantities."

"Broke? Why, Sam told me you're the best pitch-man in the country."

"I am," Johnny said, modestly. "But did Sam also tell you that he cut high card this morning for every dime we had?"

"What about you, matching for two hundred bucks?" Sam growled.

"We didn't work for that money. Which reminds me I've got to do something about the financial situation. It's nice meeting you, Miss Dalton, but—"

"Oh, I'll see you around. I've got to run now anyway. Get my hair done for this evening. . . ."

"It looks good enough now," Sam said, loyally.

She smiled at Sam, but got up. Sam waved to the bartender. "Just charge this to Room 821."

He tossed a quarter tip on the table.

Vivian Dalton went out of the cocktail lounge through the front door, to the street. Johnny turned toward the lobby door and gripped Sam's arm savagely.

"All right, now, where'd you get the dough for this tip—and that magic stuff?"

Sam grinned. "I put the bite into Eddie Miller for a fiver."

"The bell captain? Aren't you ashamed of yourself? . . ."

"Why should I be? The kid makes good dough here. . . ."

"He does, eh? Well, just a minute. . . ." Johnny left Sam near the desk and walked across the lobby to where Eddie Miller was presiding over the bell stand.

"Hi, Eddie," he said, confidentially, to the bell captain. "How's business?"

"Pretty good these days, with the fair. How's things by you, Mr. Fletcher?"

"So-so. Just getting started on a big season. Look, Eddie, how much do they pay you here?"

"Fifteen bucks a month."

"Fifteen bucks! Why! . . ."

"Oh," grinned Eddie, "the salary's just nominal. They got to pay something, by law. It's the tips. I average ten bucks a day in normal times and now, with the fair, I been running close to twenty . . . And of course, all the hops kick in a buck per day."

"Maybe I'm in the wrong racket," Johnny said.

"Nah, I've heard plenty about you, from the boys. Why, they say you've made seventy-five G's in a year, selling those books."

"I did, one year. I lost it all in the stock market."

"Easy come, easy go. That's the way with me. Maybe you don't think the nags take me for plenty."

"Sam's the horse player for us," said

Johnny. "Well, look, Eddie, I'm a little short today and I wondered if you could slip me, say, a twenty, until tomorrow?"

"Oh, sure, Mr. Fletcher. I don't mind. I wouldn't do it for regular guests, but you—I'll bring the dough up to your room. I only got silver here and Peabody might breeze in while I'm counting it out...."

"Thanks, pal. I won't forget it."

Johnny went back to Sam and they rode up to the eighth floor in the elevator. As they went into their room, Sam complained, "You shouldn't have bawled him out for lending me that five, Johnny...."

"I didn't bawl him out. I'm borrowing twenty bucks from him. You piker!"

Eddie was already tapping on the door. He brought in a fistful of half dollars and quarters. "Here you are, Mr. Fletcher."

"You're a pal, Eddie. Someday I'm going over to my friend, who's the manager of the Barbizon-Waldorf and put in a word—"

"Nix, you promised me that once before."

"That's right, I did. Come to think of it, you wouldn't want to hop bells in a snotty joint like that, anyway."

"'S all right, Mr. Fletcher. I like your style, see. You're the slickest guest ever came to this hotel and I'm a smooth bird myself. I don't use a blackjack, but there ain't one guest a month gets by here without slipping me something, see? . . ."

"I see, Eddie. Someday you'll be manager of this hotel."

"Me, manager? Nothin' doing. You know what they pay Peabody? Two fifty a month. And he don't make any tips. I make twice as much as he does."

Johnny shook his head sadly after Eddie Miller had gone. "There's no justice in this world. Look at me, one of the smartest guys who ever slicked a slicker. I'm dead broke and I've got to borrow from a bellhop. And the bellhop makes more than the manager of the hotel."

"There's nobody can make more'n you, when you pay attention to business and quit fooling around with murder cases...."

Johnny frowned. "That reminds me, did you know that talking clock isn't worth any seventy-five grand? I talked to a clock expert and he says ten thousand would be plenty for it."

"Huh? Why, we heard the Greek offer seventy-five thousand."

"And he's no chump. This clock man knows Bos and says he drives a hard bargain. So what do you make of it?"

"I dunno," said Sam. "I been thinking. What's so wonderful about a talking clock? What the hell does it say?"

Johnny stared at his friend a moment. Then he inhaled softly: "Yes, what *does* it say?"

"We heard it in the pawnshop in Columbus. It didn't say anything special. And that not too clear....

It said: 'Five o'clock and the day is nearly done.' But what does it say for the other hours? I wonder..."

"What?"

"Whether we have missed the whole point. Maybe it isn't the clock at all that's so important."

"What else could it be?"

"It could be . . . the things the clock says. . . . Look, Sam, when we were in the Quisenberry place yesterday and all the clocks went off, what happened?"

"Why, they made a racket that almost drove me nuts."

"I know that. But what else? Just before they went off. Nick Bos had offered fifty thousand bucks. When the clocks went off, he stuck his head down next to the Talking Clock. Remember? He listened to what it said and when he straightened up, he raised the ante twenty-five G's. . . . Why?"

"I don't know. I didn't hear the clock say anything. . . . Too much racket. . . ."

"For me, too. But I'm wondering, now. This Bos guy is slick. And so's Jim Partridge. For five or ten G's, he wouldn't be working so hard, but for seventy-five, or more—Say! . . ."

A strange look came over Johnny Fletcher's face. Sam, watching, stirred uneasily. "What is it, Johnny?"

"That Dalton dame. Did she pick you up or did you pick her up?"

Sam scratched his head. "Why, I was showing Eddie a couple of tricks in the lobby and she was sitting there. She laughed and then, well, one thing led to another and—"

"Okay, I can guess the rest. So she picked you up. I thought so."

"What's wrong about a doll picking me up?" Sam scowled. "After all, I'm not a gorilla and she was a swell dish."

"A swell decoy."

"Decoy? What do you mean?"

"I mean, she deliberately struck up an acquaintance with us and then what'd she do—invited us to the Lucky Seven Club. You know what, I've a good notion to take her up on that invitation."

"We can't. Not with the way our clothes look. We can get some new shirts and things, but our suits aren't so hot. Not for the Lucky Seven. If we had maybe a hundred bucks or so..."

"Clothes can be had without money. I've a good notion to try the bathroom-burglar gag on Peabody, the old skinflint."

"You mean throw your old suit out of the window, then holler that someone came into the room while you were taking a bath and swiped your suit?"

Johnny chuckled. "I haven't worked that one in five or six years. I'm afraid it wouldn't work on Peabody. He'd claim one of us took the other's clothes out and he's just mean enough to let us walk through the lobby in our shorts and shirts. No, I've got to think of something else."

Sam began muttering something about "Here we come, jail..." while Johnny sat down on the edge of the bed and copied Rodin's "Thinker."

After a moment he began to chuckle and Sam turned a frowning face upon him. "Why don't we just go down to jail right now and save them the trouble of coming after us?"

Johnny picked up the telephone and said, "Bell captain, please." Then, "Eddie Miller? This is Johnny Fletcher. Wonder if you can tell me something? Where does Mr. Peabody, the manager, buy his clothes?"

Eddie sniffed. "At Hagemann's on Broadway, near 40th. I had to take one back there for alterations for him only last week. You wouldn't want to buy there, though, Mr. Fletcher. It's a cheap joint."

"I know. I just wanted to settle an argument with Sam. I said Peabody must have bought his clothes at either Hagemann's or McGaa's. I was right."

He hung up and turned to Sam. "Run down and buy an afternoon paper. Hurry up, we're going to get some new suits."

"I don't like it," Sam said, but went out.

When he returned with the newspaper, Johnny began paging through it. "Yep, here she is—a nice full-page ad. They're featuring a blue suit with a white pin stripe at $19.85. Burlap, but better than what we're wearing now. Have you noticed, Sam, that Mr. Peabody is just about my size?"

"But *I* couldn't wear his clothes. I wear a 44 suit."

"Forty-four, eh?"

Johnny picked up the telephone, while Sam ducked into the bathroom, in order not to hear. A minute later, a man's voice in the store of Hagemann's said, gruffly:

"Harley Hagemann talking."

Johnny raised his voice two scales. "This is Mr. Peabody, manager of the 45th Street Hotel. You know that suit—bought at your store a week or so ago?"

"H'arya, Mr. Peabody. Yeah. I remember the suit. We made an alteration for you."

"That's right. Well, I had a very unfortunate experience with that suit. My uncle came to visit me here and sitting down on my desk, upset a big bottle of ink and ruined both our suits. I wonder if you could do me a personal favor, Mr. Hagemann. . . ."

"Why, certainly, Mr. Peabody. You'd like a new suit, huh?"

"Precisely. You have my measurements there. I've been looking in today's paper and I notice you're featuring a very nice blue suit, with a white pin stripe, at $19.85 . . ."

"And a steal at that price, Mr. Peabody. It's positively worth $45.00, that suit. On Fift' Avenue it'd cost you—"

"Yes, yes," Johnny cut in, mimicking Peabody's impatient tone. "I understand all that. But here's the favor. I can't leave the hotel now, and I must have a new suit for this evening. Can't you—taking my measurements—rush a suit of that style and price right over here to the hotel?"

"We certainly could, Mr. Peabody. We got it in all sizes."

"Splendid. At the same time, send over another suit, for my uncle—let's see, Uncle, you say you wear size 44? That's right, another suit of the same material, only size 44. . . . And put them both on my bill. Yes?"

Johnny squinted as he waited for the answer to the last question. If Peabody didn't have a charge account or Hagemann didn't think him worthy of a little credit, the game was up.

But Hagemann made the correct answer. "Of course, Mr. Peabody. I'll put it on your bill. . . . How soon you want the suits?"

"Immediately. I may not be in the office when the boy brings them, but just leave them at the desk for me."

Johnny hung up and called to Sam. "Quick Sam, run across the street to the haberdashers and buy us each a nice shirt . . . and on the way back, pick up a white carnation."

"Why the carnation?"

"Peabody always wears one, doesn't he? And so do most of the hotel clerks. It's just like a badge . . . Hurry! . . ."

Johnny took a quick shower, while Sam got the shirts. When Sam returned, Johnny took the pins out of his shirt and put it on. The white carnation he carefully put into his breast pocket.

"Now," he said to Sam, "Hagemann's is on Broadway, near 40th. They'll send the messenger here with the suits. It's your job to get outside the hotel and take up a post about fifty feet up the street. When you see someone with two suit boxes, or a big box that might contain two suits, you take a quick gander and make sure the name Hagemann is on the box, then you run ahead into the hotel and give me the high sign. I need thirty seconds to get out the white carnation and set the stage. Understand? . . . You can't miss up."

"Oh, I'll do it," groaned Sam. "But there's going to be hell to pay when Peabody gets his bill. He'll suspect us, right off the bat. . . ."

"No, he won't. Because in a day or two, after I get forty bucks, I'm going to step down to Hagemann's and pay them for our suits. Or I'll send Eddie Miller down with the money. Peabody need never know that we used his credit. . . ."

They went downstairs and Johnny

seated himself in the lobby near the door. Sam went outside.

Peabody was nowhere in sight.

Eddie Miller strolled over. "The boss just stuck a French Key in a guy's room on the fourth floor. The poor guy owed only three weeks' rent."

Johnny shuddered. "Thanks for telling me, Eddie. I don't feel so bad now."

Sam Cragg burst into the hotel, saw Johnny and headed for the elevator. Johnny got up quickly, took the carnation out of his pocket and put it into his lapel. Then he started toward the door.

When he was six feet from it, a pimply-faced youth of about nineteen, carrying two suit boxes, came in.

"Ah," Johnny exclaimed. "Here you are—from Hagemann's!"

"You Mr. Peabody? . . ." mumbled the youth.

"Of course! Tell Mr. Hagemann I appreciate the quick service. And here, my boy, is a half dollar for you." Loftily he dropped the coin into the boy's hand.

He turned away and just then one of

the elevators opened and Mr. Peabody, white carnation and all, stepped out.

"Ha! Mr. Fletcher," he said. "Been buying some clothes? . . . You must be prosperous. Mmm, Hagemann's; a good store."

"Only fair, Mr. Peabody, only fair. I just wanted a knock-about or two and my Park Avenue tailor . . ." He let the words trail off and stepped past Mr. Peabody into the elevator.

Upstairs, in Room 821, Sam Cragg was perspiring freely. "It worked!" he cried, in relief.

"Of course it worked. My stunts always work . . . well, almost always." He chuckled. "I bumped into Peabody. You know, I'm tempted to let the suits go through on his bill. . . ."

"No!" howled Sam. "The first of the month is only three days off."

"Right you are, but all day I've heard the faint whisper of far-off money. . . and the sound is coming closer."

"I hope so, Johnny, I hope so. Things been tough too long."

17

AND so that evening, nicely shaved, shoes shined, their hair trimmed and wearing the new clothes, Johnny Fletcher and Sam Cragg entered the Lucky Seven Club.

The headwaiter showed them to a table, not too far from the handkerchief-sized dance floor, and when the waiter came, Johnny ordered. "Two bottles of beer . . . and a bowl of pretzels!"

"Beg pardon, sir," said the waiter, "you know there's a $3.00 minimum?"

"Ha? And how much is a bottle of beer?"

"One dollar, sir!"

"All right, we'll have a couple of bottles later to make up the minimum."

"Don't look now, Johnny," whispered Sam "but isn't that the clock fella over there by the wall? . . ."

Johnny twisted his head. He smiled and

nodded to Wilbur Tamarack. The latter looked puzzled for a moment, then his face broke in recognition.

"Sit here and watch our beers, Sam."

Johnny got up and worked his way to the table, where Tamarack was seated with a girl wearing a white fox evening cape. The girl's back had been toward Johnny, but when he came up he was astonished to see that it was Diana Rusk. Somehow, he hadn't expected her to go to a night club so soon after her husband's death.

"Well, well!" he exclaimed.

"Hello, Fletcher," Tamarack said shortly.

Diana Rusk was more cordial. "Mr. Fletcher. Won't you . . . join us?"

"Sam is holding down a table for us. Later, perhaps you might dance?"

A slight frown creased her forehead. "Perhaps . . ."

Johnny nodded. "How's the clock business, Mr. Tamarack?"

"Fine. And your . . . business?"

"Ticking. . . . See you later."

Johnny returned to his table to find that Sam had already guzzled most of one bottle of beer. "After this afternoon, this is a let down," Sam complained.

"Maybe your girl friend will pick you up? Where is she?"

"I asked the waiter. She goes on in a minute."

The drummer in the orchestra rolled his drum and the master of ceremonies was focused into a spotlight.

"Ladies and gentlemen," he announced, "I give you that popular song stylist, Miss . . . Vivian Dalton!"

Vivian Dalton, wearing a white evening gown that revealed plenty, walked into the spotlight. She had an excellent voice, low and throaty, with a catch to it now and then that caused a little ripple to race up and down Johnny's spine.

"Say, ain't she swell?" Sam Cragg whispered across the table.

Johnny nodded. "Shut up, I want to hear her."

She had caught his eyes now and gave him a half sad smile. His pulse began to throb slowly and for the moment he forgot that he had suspected Vivian Dalton of being a decoy.

She finished the song, amid tremendous applause, then sang "The Gaucho Serenade" for an encore. When she left the floor, a trio of tap dancers came on.

Johnny relaxed. "Not bad. A girl like that could cut your throat and you wouldn't even mind it."

"I think you're wrong about her, Johnny," said Sam. "For my money she's okay."

"What money?"

"Shh! Here she comes."

Johnny pushed back his chair quickly. Vivian Dalton came slowly toward them, smiling tantalizingly. "Hi, boys," she greeted them. "I see you came anyway."

"How, you'll never know." Johnny grinned. "You're pretty good, you know."

"You haven't seen any Hollywood talent scouts knocking me over, have you?"

Johnny pulled up a vacant chair from

an adjoining table. "Sit down a while, won't you?"

"For a minute."

"And how about a bottle of beer?"

"Beer?"

"We're on a budget. Besides beer is healthy. With a voice like yours, you've got to—" He stopped for Vivian Dalton was staring past him.

He turned, just as Sam Cragg exclaimed: "Jeez, Partridge and—Look! . . ."

It was Jim Partridge. Jim Partridge in evening clothes and with—Bonita Quisenberry.

"Oh-*oh!*" Johnny breathed. Then he looked up quickly at Vivian Dalton. "Ah, so *he's* the one."

She shook her head as if to clear it of a haze. 'What?"

"You know Jim Partridge."

"Yes, I know him. I also know . . ." She laughed, shortly. "Dalton is my stage name. It used to be . . . Partridge."

Johnny almost knocked over his glass

of beer. Sam Cragg whistled in astonishment. "Your husband!"

"Husband? How old do you think I am? He's . . . my father!"

"And Bonita?" gasped Johnny.

She nodded. "I haven't seen her since the divorce, seven years ago, when I was thirteen. I didn't know . . ."

"That they'd made up? Neither did I."

Vivian got up suddenly. "I must change for my next number. Excuse me. . . ."

When she had gone, Johnny pushed back his own chair. "Hold the fort, Sam. I want a word with Partridge."

"Holler if he gets rough."

Partridge had already seen Johnny. He said something to Bonita as Johnny approached and she turned and watched him with an expression of distaste on her sulky face.

"Hello, pal," Johnny said, easily, as he stopped beside Partridge's table.

"You've got your neck washed," Partridge said, sarcastically.

"I washed it for you. It's sticking out."

"Must you talk to this man, Jim?" Bonita asked sharply. "You said you would leave your work at the office."

"Did I say that?" Partridge asked, coolly. "I don't remember. That's why I've been trying to get a stake."

"Well, you've got it now." Johnny looked at Bonita.

Partridge shook his head, slowly. "You're slipping, fella. The game's one move farther ahead. Buy a paper when you leave."

"Something bust?"

"So long, Fletcher," Partridge said, pointedly. "I'm dealing you out."

Johnny retreated to his table, his face screwed up in thought. That Bonita had thrown in with Partridge was a significant development, but Partridge was referring to something else . . . something that he expected to be printed in the papers. But he wasn't telling. He had arranged for Johnny to be here at the Lucky Seven this evening, but in the interim something had happened and he no longer needed Johnny.

Why had he needed him in the first place?

"What's up, Johnny?" asked Sam.

"Something. I don't know what."

"The Rusk kid's been looking over here. I think she wants to talk to you."

"They all do," Johnny said, unhappily. "They want to scratch dirt over me. I've been sleeping and they're burying me. Well...."

The tap dancers had finished and the orchestra was playing a dance number. Couples were moving onto the tiny dance floor. Johnny went over to the Rusk–Tamarack table. "Are you ready to try that dance, Miss Rusk?" he asked, stiffly.

She got up and he led her to the floor. Johnny hadn't danced in almost three years, but it made no difference. No one else was dancing. They couldn't, on that crowded little floor. They merely shuffled and swayed.

"I saw you talking to Bonita," Diana Rusk said into Johnny's ear as they began to shuffle. "Did you know that she left Twelve O'Clock House this afternoon?"

"Ah! Tit for tat. Did you know that the man with her is Jim Partridge, her ex-husband?"

He felt shock ripple through her body. "I don't understand. I thought she and . . . Cornish . . . Eric discharged Cornish this morning and when she left later . . ."

"I'll tell you something else," said Johnny, deliberately. "The girl who sang a while ago—Vivian Dalton—she's the daughter of Jim and Bonita Partridge."

"Why, I didn't know she had a daughter! Eric never told Mo—"

"Your mother? Maybe Bonita forgot to tell Eric. It seems Jim raised her, after the divorce. Or she raised Jim. It's a question. Imagine a cheap, second-rate private detective having a daughter like that."

She was silent a moment, then said, "I suppose you wondered why I came to a place like this, after . . ."

"No," he said, "I wasn't wondering. You hadn't seen the Kid in months. . . ."

"Oh, it's not that. I—you've caught me a couple of times today. You know about

Mother and Eric. Well, during the quarrel between Eric and Bonita there was a telephone call for her and he overheard her agree to meet someone at this place."

Johnny screwed up his face. "He asked you to come here and find out who she was meeting?"

"Oh, no! Eric wouldn't do a thing like that. He just happened to let it drop talking to Mother. Coming was my own idea. You see . . . I decided I wanted that clock, after all."

"Ah! You figure if anyone stole it, it was Bonita?"

"Why not? That's all she was waiting around for . . . money! I didn't particularly want the clock myself, but I most certainly didn't want Bonita to have it. You probably know that I don't care much for her. I blame her for . . . for Tommy's running off."

"She made it warm for him at home?"

"Warm is a mild word. She knew that Tommy was his grandfather's favorite and she tried her best to estrange them. Then after Tommy left, she started in on Eric. And—and all the while she was carrying on with that estate manager, Cornish."

"Cornish seems to have lost out," Johnny remarked. "Either that or Jim Partridge has smelled out some money somewhere and she wants to get in on it. Partridge is a very capable customer. I'm waiting for him to pull a rabbit out of the hat right now. Sam and I are here tonight because of him. At least, I think so...."

At that moment the music stopped. Johnny took Diana's arm and led her back to where Tamarack was sitting at their table. The sales manager of the Quisenberry Clock Company had his elbows propped up on the table and his chin in his cupped hands.

He did not get up. "Sit down a minute, Fletcher," he invited, sullenly. "I'd like to have you tell me about your game."

"Game, Mr. Tamarack?" Johnny asked, mockingly. "I'm not playing any games."

"Then what *are* you doing? Wasn't that a game, coming down to the office, pretending to be a big clock buyer from out west? You're not a detective, so why should you be interested in all this?"

Johnny pulled up a chair from an adjoining table and seated himself.

"Look, Tamarack," he said, seriously, "I met Tom Quisenberry up in Minnesota. I got to like him and he trusted me. He'd had some tough breaks, but he got a worse one—he lost his life. I'm playing this game, as you call it, because I think I can bring to justice the person who killed Tom Quisenberry...."

"But you and your friend claimed that a tramp had killed Tom. That Minnesota tramp would hardly be here in New York, would he?"

"Why not? The Talking Clock's here. That man who was disguised as a tramp—"

"Whoa!" exclaimed Tamarack. "You're not going to say that the tramp wasn't a tramp at all, but someone close to the Quisenberry family, disguised as a tramp?..."

"I was going to say exactly that. What's wrong with it?"

Wilbur Tamarack cocked his head to one side and looked derisively at Johnny. Then he turned to Diana Rusk, who was staring at Johnny, her lips pressed into a thin, straight line.

"What do *you* think, Diana?"

She shook her head. "I don't know what to think. But I do know that I met Mr. Fletcher in Minnesota and I've a pretty fair idea of what he went through to get from there to here, just to . . . just to give me something that he thought belonged to me."

"Thanks," said Johnny. He got up.

Wilbur Tamarack's face reddened down to the line of his collar. "I didn't know you felt like that about it, Diana."

"I do. Now you know."

Johnny smiled at her and turned away. Then he wheeled back. "That heavy-set fellow just coming; that's Lieutenant Madigan of the Homicide Squad. I'm afraid he's here on business. . . . If I were you, I'd clear out!"

He smiled and walked briskly back to his own table.

"Get under the table, Sam! An old friend's just come in."

Sam ducked low and almost did get down under the table. "'S too late," Johnny muttered.

He pretended to see the detective for the first time. "The house is pinched! It's Lieutenant Madigan..."

"Fletcher! And Cragg! I thought you birds had gone out into the Bible belt to scalp the natives."

Johnny shook hands with the detective. "They scalped us, pal."

"You don't look it. You must be holding heavy, hanging around night clubs."

Johnny winked. "If you only knew...."

"Don't tell me. I've got enough troubles now. Mmm, there's my customer."

"You mean Jim Partridge?"

Lieutenant Madigan, turning away,

whirled back on Johnny. "You know Partridge?"

"Uh-huh. His wife, too. I mean ex-wife. That's her with him."

A look of consternation spread across the detective's face. "Don't tell me," he whispered. "Don't tell me that *you're* mixed in the Quisenberry case?"

Johnny looked down at his hands. "I was figuring on solving the case . . . for you."

Lieutenant Madigan blinked as if an invisible fist had struck him in the face. "I don't know why these things happen to me. I only got in this by accident, because the chief of police of Hillcrest happens to be an old buddy and he called me up and asked me as a personal favor to look into some things here in the city. And now I find that you're in it, knee deep. . . . All right, what do you know? Partridge will hold a minute."

He sat down heavily in the chair that had been used recently by Vivian Dalton.

"Why," said Johnny. "I could tell a

better story if you would tell me what's happened this evening."

"What makes you think anything's happened?"

"Because Partridge told me so less than ten minutes ago. Said I'd be reading it in the papers."

"Well, it's out already, so I'll tell you. The Quisenberry estate manager, a fella named Cornish, has been knocked off."

Johnny inhaled. "Where?"

"On the place."

"How long ago? That's important, Madigan."

"His body was found early in the evening, in his cottage, but he'd apparently been shot sometime during the afternoon. Early afternoon."

Johnny frowned. "Then the alibis are no good."

"Partridge's? Not if you mean his being here this evening. Nor his wife's. Merryman—that's my buddy in Hillcrest—says he's questioned Eric Quisenberry. Quisenberry says his wife left him around noon, after a spat. He admitted that she had been friendly with this Cornish and that the argument had been partly because of him. In fact, he'd given Cornish his walking papers. It's Quisenberry's frau I want to talk to. And Partridge . . . and I'd better grab them. They're getting ready to leave."

He got up quickly and walked toward Partridge's table, Johnny following at his heels.

"Hello, Partridge," Madigan said. "How's tricks?"

Partridge's face was stony, but there was a gleam in his eyes as he looked from Madigan to Johnny.

"Hello, Madigan," he said. "I see the punk's talked to you."

"Punk?" exclaimed Johnny. "Why the Lieutenant and I are practically pals. I help him solve his cases. The tough ones."

Lieutenant Madigan grunted. "You know what happened in Hillcrest? And you, Mrs. Quisenberry?"

Bonita Quisenberry's face was like old ivory, yellow and hard.

Before she could speak, Jim Partridge said, harshly:

"So the punk's a pal of yours, Lieutenant, eh? He covered the Rusk girl's escape. They were dancing together when you came in."

Madigan turned to Johnny. "That right, Fletcher?"

"Was I dancing with Miss Rusk? Why, yes. But I didn't know you were interested in her. I didn't even *know* why you were coming in."

"You! . . ." Madigan said, bitterly.

"She was with Wilbur Tamarack, the manager of the Quisenberry Clock Company," Partridge went on. "And Tamarack's a lad who'll stand some questioning himself. . . . What do you want with me, Lieutenant?"

"Where were you this afternoon?"

"In my office. All afternoon."

"And you've got the office help to prove it? I know."

Partridge smiled thinly. "Can you prove I wasn't in the office?"

"Of course I can't. . . . Let's get out of here. People are beginning to look."

Johnny went back to his table and called for his check. The waiter figured a while and gave it to him. Johnny howled. "Whaddya mean, twelve dollars? I only had one bottle of beer."

"So sorry," said the waiter, giving Johnny a venomous look. "I'll check up." He went off and got into a huddle with another waiter. When he came back he corrected the bill. "It's six dollars, sir, the *minimum* charge for two."

Johnny counted out six dollars in silver, then added an extra quarter.

The waiter picked up the quarter from the tray. "What's this, sir?"

"My breakfast money," snarled Johnny, snatching the coin from the man's hand. "And now you can whistle for your tip."

"Thank you sir. Come again soon, I hope not."

"Six bucks for two bottles of beer," muttered Sam Cragg as he followed

Johnny to the door where Madigan and the others were waiting.

When they reached the sidewalk, Johnny said to Madigan, "Will you be wanting to talk to me some more this evening, Maddy?"

Madigan chewed at his lower lip. He looked at Bonita Quisenberry and her former husband. Then he shook his head. "I'll be busy for a couple of hours and I'd just as soon not have you around. Where you staying—that rat's nest on 45th Street? Or Park Avenue?"

"Forty-fifth Street. I'll put a lamp in the window in case you should come prowling around later."

"Okay. And if I don't show up, stick around in the morning. I'll want to talk to you then."

"Fine."

As they walked down Sixth Avenue, Sam Cragg said, "if you ask me, Partridge did it. You practically told him that his ex was carrying on with this Cornish lad."

Johnny shook his head. "Cornish was a surly monkey. Let's step into this drugstore here a minute. I want to make a telephone call."

"Who you going to call at this time of the night?"

"La Guardia. I want to tell him there's a fire somewhere. . . ."

He went into the drugstore and entered a phone booth. Dialing the operator, he was informed that a call to Hillcrest would cost him twenty cents. He dropped the coins into the slot. A moment later he said: "Hello, is this the chief of police of Hillcrest? This is the Homicide Squad of New York. Lieutenant Madigan just told me to call you and ask a question about the Cornish murder. . . ."

"He's got something?" the Hillcrest chief exclaimed.

"I don't know. He's still out. He telephoned in to say he's picked up those people. What he wanted me to find out for him was about this man, Cornish. Was there a piece of adhesive tape on his face when you looked him over?"

"Why, yes," replied the chief. "That was something I meant to tell Madigan about. The tape was on the face, but there wasn't any cut or bruise under it. Which was funny, because the night before Cornish claimed to have had a fight with some burglars. . . . Tell Madigan about that and have him telephone me himself when he comes in."

"I will. Thanks."

Johnny hung up and rejoined Sam. As they left the store, he said: "Cornish swiped the Talking Clock himself. And the person who killed him got it away from him today."

"I still say Partridge," Sam Cragg said, doggedly.

"I say no," Johnny replied.

They were still arguing about it when they turned into the 45th Street Hotel. And there, Mort Murray, haggard, unshaven, got up from a chair in the lobby.

"Mort!" exclaimed Johnny. "What're you doing here so late in the evening?"

"Didn't Sam tell you I was coming here?" Mort asked, bitterly.

Sam winced. "I did mention it to Johnny."

"That's right, he did. But something . . . uh, something came up. What's on your mind, Mort?"

Mort's eyes roamed over the new suits that Johnny and Sam were wearing. "You know what, Johnny. That loan shark. You promised—"

"That's right, I did. Come upstairs, Mort, and we'll talk it over."

When they entered Room 821, Johnny turned to Mort. "I guess Sam told you about our little bad luck. Why we didn't come over to your place this morning? . . ."

"Sam told me. But did he tell you that Carmella, the loan shark, came in while he was there and made all sorts of threats, because I didn't have the interest money for him?"

"I never got to tell him that," Sam scowled.

Mort's eyes were disillusioned. "You know what he did? He fined me twenty-five percent. I owe a hundred and fifty dollars now, plus the interest, which'll be twenty dollars tomorrow. And if I don't pay the interest, I get fined another twenty-five percent."

"Why, the dirty—!" Johnny swore. "He can't do that."

"He can't, eh? You come over tomorrow and tell him that he can't. I tell you, I'm sunk if I don't get some money tomorrow. The interest money, at least."

Johnny went through his pockets. He found less than seven dollars. "How much have you got Sam?"

Sam shelled out a dollar and a half. "Those shirts and things we bought...."

"I know. All right, get Eddie Miller on the phone."

"Can't, he's off this evening. But he'll be on at seven in the morning."

"Okay, we'll nick him for twenty bucks the first thing in the morning. That'll take care of Mort's interest money in the morning. And sometime during the day I'll rustle up some more money for you, Mort."

"Thanks, Johnny. I knew you'd come across."

"Sure, don't I always? Now, what about a place to sleep tonight?"

"I was figuring on sleeping in the office."

"You won't have to do that. Sam'll share his bed with you. Save you coming back in the morning. Let's turn in now, fellows; we've got a big day ahead."

18

THE sun shining on his face woke Johnny Fletcher in the morning. He lay for a moment, looking at the two mounds on the bed beyond, then he whistled and sat up.

"Up, boys! It's morning."

He sprang out of bed and headed for the bathroom. When he came out later, shaved and whistling, Sam Cragg and Mort Murray were partially dressed.

"It's after eight, Johnny," Mort reminded. "Think you ought to call that bellboy?"

"Righto!" Johnny went to the phone and got Eddie Miller and asked him to come up. When the bell captain came into the room, he looked cynically at Mort Murray.

"Ringing in an extra sleeper, Mr. Fletcher? Peabody ain't going to like that."

"Lots of things Peabody doesn't like, Eddie, my boy. This is a pal of mine and he's in a jam. Unless I can, uh, lend him twenty bucks this morning, things are going to happen to him. So, Eddie—"

"Jeez, Mr. Fletcher! I had to borrow carfare this morning. You know what? I got in a kelly pool game with a couple sharks last night and they cleaned me."

Mort Murray groaned and the light went out of Johnny's eyes. "Eddie," he said, sadly, "you disappoint me. If you must play kelly pool why don't you play it with Sam here some time? He was the three-cushion champ of Bremer County, Iowa, once. Well, when do you think you can get twenty bucks?"

"Not before night, and maybe not then if things is slow today. You know, Mr. Fletcher, I'd give it to you if I had it. The shirt off my back!"

"That goes for me, too, Eddie."

Eddie moved regretfully to the door. There he paused. "Say, Fletcher, how'd you and Sam get the new suits, if you was broke?"

Johnny waggled a finger at the bellboy. "That's a secret, Eddie. A secret I hope no one'll ever know."

Eddie nodded, but there was a speculative gleam in his eye as he went out.

There was a film of perspiration on Mort's face. "Jeez, I can't go to the office. Carmella'll be waitin' there for me."

"Sam'll go with you. In fact, I'll go myself, Mort, old boy...."

The door panels almost cracked under the pounding of a heavy fist. Then the door was flung open and Lieutenant Madigan strode in.

"Did I wake you up?"

"If I'd been dead you'd woke me up," retorted Johnny. Then his face twisted into a grin. "But you're welcome as the flowers in May. Look, Lieutenant, this is Mort Murray, as fine a lad as you'd find anywhere in this big city. He's a book publisher. In fact, he publishes that little gem, *Every Man A Samson*, with which I've been making a living, such as it be, for the last ten years. And now, he's in

Dutch. He got into the clutches of a loan shark."

"'S tough," sympathized Madigan. "What's his name?"

"Carmella, ah! That means Nick. . . ."

"Nick who?" Johnny asked.

"Nick Bosapopolous, or something. He calls himself Nick Bos for short."

"Nick Bos, did you say?" Johnny howled.

"Yeah, he controls half the loan-shark business in this burg. Everybody knows that, for all the good it does us. . . ."

"Nick Bos, the sponge man, down on West Avenue?"

Lieutenant Madigan shrugged. "I guess he's got a sponge business or something as a blind."

"Holy Donald Duck!" cried Sam Cragg.

Johnny sat down heavily on his bed. "So that's how he can afford seventy-five thousand dollars for a clock!"

"Huh?" said Lieutenant Madigan.

"Didn't the Partridges mention him

when you questioned them? Hell, Bos is knee-deep in the Quisenberry business."

Lieutenant Madigan turned red in the face. "They didn't say a word about him. They didn't say much of anything. Partridge stuck to his alibi and the Quisenberry dame kept hollering for a lawyer. I finally turned them loose. Now, you talk, Fletcher. How's Bos in this?"

"Let's," said Johnny, "go down and talk to him. Right now."

"Suits me, we can have a chin on the way down. I got the limousine out front."

Sam and Mort finished dressing and then they all left the room. In the lobby, Mr. Peabody was running his fingers over the seams of the furniture to see if the cleaners had missed any dust. He exclaimed when he saw Lieutenant Madigan.

"I knew it, Fletcher! You're in trouble again."

"You hope, Peabody! This isn't a pinch. And I'll thank you not to make slanderous remarks in hotel lobbies." Johnny headed for the door, muttering to himself . . . "Only two days to the first. Will *he* be surprised!"

Detective Fox sat behind the wheel of the limousine. He knew Johnny and Sam from other days, but did not greet them with any great enthusiasm. Mort climbed in beside Detective Fox and the others got in back.

Madigan gave Fox the address of Bos' office. As the car headed westward toward the express highway, he said to Johnny:

"My friend, Merryman in Hillcrest, called me this morning. Some bird claiming to be from the department called him last night . . . right after you left the Lucky Seven. What's the angle, Fletcher?"

"Joe Cornish claimed he had a fight the night before with some burglars—when the Talking Clock was swiped. When I saw him yesterday he had some adhesive tape stuck on his face. Merryman said it was a dummy. Catch on?"

"Yeah! Cornish didn't fight with burglars? So he swiped the clock himself?"

"I'd figured Bonita for it, at first. She wanted to sell it to Bos for seventy-five G's on account of Old Simple Simon died broke and didn't leave her husband any dough."

"Why should she swipe the clock, when her husband was getting it anyway?"

"That's it; he wasn't. The clock went to the Rusk kid. It seems the old man had given it outright to his grandson, Tom Quisenberry, who was killed up in —I mean who died before the old man. The kid was married to Diana, so the clock belongs to her."

"Why don't people tell me these things?" exclaimed Madigan.

"Why don't you ask around like me? So since I'm asking, how was this Cornish killed?"

"The popular way; a bullet. A .32. Right behind the ear."

"A small gun," grunted Johnny. "And behind the ear. Mmm."

"It *could* be the dame. Well, I got a

couple of men on her. She's checked in at the Sorenson...."

"Partridge lives there himself."

"I know; but they're on different floors. I got a couple of men on Partridge, too. And ... uh, Merryman's talking to the girl out in Hillcrest. Which reminds me, that was a dirty trick of yours letting her slip by me last night. I got the fella though ... Tamarack."

"Where?"

"Oh, I was laying for him when he got to his apartment on East 57th. That's how come I didn't get around to you. He didn't show up until 3 a.m. Drove the girl all the way out to Hillcrest. What do you make of Tamarack?"

Johnny shrugged. "He's got a crush on that girl. With the Kid out of the way, he may win out, now."

"He told me he's practically run the clock factory the last two years. But Eric gave him his notice yesterday."

"Eric? I'll be damned. The mouse has become a tomcat. First he told off his wife, then he fired his old man's pet.

Looks like he's going to take hold of things."

Detective Fox said, over his shoulder. "Here we are, Lieutenant, but—Jeez, you know what place this is?"

"I know, Fox. Stop the car behind the big Cadillac."

Fox obeyed and they climbed out of the limousine. Johnny walked forward to the limousine and looked at the mongram on the door. "NB" he commented.

"So what's it to you?" snapped the heavy-jowled man sitting behind the wheel.

Lieutenant Madigan looked at Detective Fox and jerked his head in the direction of the tough chauffeur. As Detective Fox walked forward, Madigan and the others entered the office of the sponge company.

The girl with the Roquefort-cheese complexion regarded the group uneasily. Her hands fluttered and went under her desk.

"Go ahead," grunted Madigan. "Give him the signal. We'll just breeze in."

They did and when they entered Nicholas Bos' office, the sponge man was leaning back comfortably in his upholstered chair, manicured fingers making a tent of his hands.

"Good morning, Lieutenant Mad'gan," he said pleasantly. "And my friends the private detectives. You have find the clock for me?"

"We'll talk about that in a minute, Bos," said Johnny, heading off the detective. "That's another little matter I want to clear up. You got a punk named Carmella working for you?"

"Carmella? I don't knowing the name."

"He's one of your collectors. He made a small loan to my pal here and he's been bothering him since."

"Collector?" said Bos. "Loan? What is this Carmella?"

"You know what he is," Madigan cut in. "One of your strong-arm punks."

A sad look came over Bos' face. "Mr. Lieutenant, You make refer to that old trouble. Ah! the deestrict attorney he say nothing, because he can prove nothing. I am sponge importer. That's all. I make a leetle money and I buy the clock, for hobby, because I am liking clock very much. That's all. I don't bother nobody and I have good friend all over. . . ."

"You've got friends," said Madigan, ominously. "Don't I know you've got friends. In the right places. But there's some things about which your friends can't help you. And murder's one of them—"

"Wait a minute!" snapped Johnny. "One thing at a time. Mort's getting cold chills by the minute, thinking about that punk Carmella. Look, Bos, Mort Murray borrowed a hundred and twenty bucks from Carmella. I want you to call off Carmella. . . . You can take the dough out of my retainer. 'Member? . . ."

Bos shrugged expressively. "All right, I don't knowing this Carmella man, but if I do knowing him I telling him, hokay, lay off Mor' Murray. Now, what's this murder business? . . ."

Johnny tapped Mort on the arm.

"Okay, pal, you can run along now. You're squared off. I'll see you later."

Sighing heavily, Mort took his departure.

Then Johnny turned again to Nicholas Bos. "You've read the morning papers and you know about Joe Cornish...."

"Is bad. Why somebody killing watchman?"

"I was going to ask that," snapped Lieutenant Madigan. "I understand you're in this up to your neck. You've made a fancy offer for a certain Talking Clock."

"Sure, I telling you. I like clock and this is very good, old clock. I wanting have him for my hobby. I also buying many other clock." Bos waved a manicured hand around his office, to indicate the clocks.

"This isn't getting us anywhere," said Madigan, angrily. "If you won't talk here, Bos, we'll go down to Headquarters."

"Sure. You got warrant? I'm thinking all this happen in Wes 'chester County."

"I'm working with the Westchester

police and I can get a warrant easily enough. You know I can. Where were you yesterday afternoon, Bos?"

"Right here in my office. I am working . . ."

Madigan's forehead creased. "I was a chump to even ask that question. You wouldn't soil your hands, anyway. And you've got so many thugs working for you it'd take me a month to round them all up. I'll start over. . . . Why do you want this particular Talking Clock?"

"I'll ask a question," Johnny Fletcher cut in. He leaned forward. *"What does the Talking Clock say at three o'clock?"*

That was the first time Johnny saw any emotion on Nicholas Bos' face. The olive complexion of the importer loan-shark actually became two shades lighter.

"I—I don't knowing what she say," he stammered.

Johnny nodded quietly and half turned to the door.

"Guess we're wasting our time, Lieutenant."

Madigan backed away reluctantly. He

sighed, wearily. "Okay. I'll be seeing you later, Bos."

Outside, the chauffeur of the Cadillac was dabbing a handkerchief at his nose. Detective Fox was leaning against the police limousine, rubbing the knuckles of his right fist.

Madigan headed for the car, but Johnny held back. "Guess I'll be leaving you here, Lieutenant."

"What for?"

"I still have to make a living, you know. Thought I'd go and sell a few books."

"You've got something up your sleeve. It's about that clock. I saw Bos' face when you asked him what the clock said at three o'clock. . . ."

The police radio, in the limousine, said suddenly: "Lieutenant Madigan, call in. Lieutenant Madigan, call in."

Madigan opened the door of the limousine and reaching in, flicked a switch. "Madigan talking, what is it?"

"Merryman of Hillcrest telephoned,"

replied the radio voice. "The Talking Clock has been returned."

"What?" exclaimed Madigan, then he switched off the radio and pulled out of the car. "Okay, Fletcher, run along."

Johnny Fletcher scowled, then signaled to Sam Cragg. They walked leisurely to the corner, then rounding it, Johnny broke into a run for a cigar store across the street. When Sam caught up to him, Johnny was already inside a telephone booth, stuffing nickels into the slot.

A moment later he was speaking to a servant in the Quisenberry home. "I want to talk to Eric Quisenberry. Tell him it's Johnny Fletcher calling."

It was a long moment before Eric Quisenberry's voice came over the telephone. "Yes, Mr. Fletcher?"

"I just learned from the New York police that the Talking Clock has been returned. How was it returned, Mr. Quisenberry?"

"Why, that's the surprising thing, Mr. Fletcher. I don't know. It most certainly was gone yesterday—from the safe. But this morning when I went into the clock room, there it was, standing amidst all the other clocks. I notified the police immediately. They—well they're here now."

"Oh!" Johnny bit his lip. Then, "Mr. Quisenberry, do you plan on going down to your office today?"

"Why, yes. In fact, I'm going to leave as soon as I finish with the police."

"Good. I'll drop in at your office sometime during the afternoon. I think . . . I'll have something important to tell you at that time."

"What? I mean, why are you taking such an interest in this? You're not—"

"I'm an old friend of Tom's, that's why. I'll see you later, Mr. Quisenberry."

He hung up abruptly. As they left the store, Sam Cragg groused, "That's screwy, the crook returning the clock, after killing a man for it."

"You're telling me, Sam? It's not only screwy, it's impossible. I don't believe it. Unless . . . the clock was never swiped at all."

"Huh? You think Quisenberry's the guy? Say—why couldn't he be?"

"He could. Eric's gotten a grip on himself. He tossed out his wife yesterday and gave the grand bounce to the Tamarack lad at the factory. Two things he never had nerve enough to do before. I wonder . . . if the clock-stealing stuff wasn't just some business to bring things to a head with Bonita. I've underestimated the guy."

"He's been sweet on the Rusk kid's mother. She looks like a dame who's got some steel in her backbone."

"Maybe she stuck a ramrod down his back. Still . . . Taxi!"

"Taxis again?" exclaimed Sam. "With the bankroll the way it is?"

"There's more where this came from. Driver, take us to Lexington and 60th."

19

TWENTY minutes later, Johnny paid the cabby a dollar and forty cents to Sam Cragg's discomfiture.

"What's up here that's worth a buck forty?" he griped.

"The clock shop across the street. You wait here. I'm going in alone."

Johnny crossed the street and entered the antique clock dealer's shop. The proprietor exclaimed when he recognized Johnny.

"You have come back, eh? What do you want today?"

"Why, I thought I'd get some additional information on clocks. For that article, you know...."

"What article? What newspaper? Yesterday, after you left I thought about something interesting to tell you for that story and I called the *Blade*. You know what they told me?"

Johnny grimaced. "That I wasn't working for them. Okay, I'll come clean. I'm a detective, working on the Quisenberry case."

"Why didn't you say so yesterday? The other man did."

"What other man?"

"The detective who was here in the afternoon. He didn't give his name."

"What'd he look like?"

The clock dealer shrugged. "How does a detective look? He didn't wear a uniform."

"What'd he want to know?"

"Don't you know? Ain't he from your office?"

"There're a half dozen of us working on the case. It was probably Snodgrass who was here. Look, you told me yesterday you'd seen this clock on exhibition. I suppose you heard it talk, too?"

"Of course. It wasn't a very good voice. Too tinny."

"I've heard it once. I'm interested in knowing *what* the clock said, not how it said it. Would you remember any of the things it said, at the different hours? Three o'clock for example?"

The clock dealer screwed up his face. "I don't remember anything particular. I heard it talk several different times. It wasn't anything unusual. Platitudes."

Johnny sighed. "Maybe I can refresh your memory. At five o'clock, the little man comes out and says: 'Five o'clock and the day is nearly done ' . . ."

"Yes, that's the kind of stuff it says. Right after that, at six o'clock, it says something about 'When the day is done and night begins to fall'."

"And at three o'clock?" Johnny leaned forward, eagerly. "Try and remember that hour, will you? . . ."

"I can't. I never paid any particular attention. Six o'clock was easy because that's considered the end of the day and you have reminded me of what the clock said then, by quoting the five o'clock recitation. But . . ."

"Yes?"

The dealer snapped his fingers. "I may have it here! Yes! I remember now, the convention special reported it the last time Simon exhibited the clock, two years ago. I've got the magazines around here."

He headed for the back of the room and opened a closet. "Yes, here they are. Copies of the *American Hobbyist*, for the last two years."

Johnny flanked the counter. "Can I help you look?"

"Yes. Let's see, the convention two years ago was in summer. July, I think. The report would be in the August issue. Look for August, 1938...."

The dealer scooped out a stack of the magazines and they began to rummage through them. It was Johnny who found the August, 1938, issue.

"Here it is!"

They spread the magazine out on the counter, their eager fingers turning the pages.

"Clock Exhibit!" read the dealer. "Here it is.... yes, 'Simon Quisenberry's Talking Clock.' At twelve o'clock it says: 'Twelve o'clock. High noon and midnight. Rest ye weary....'"

"Three o'clock!" exclaimed Johnny. "'Three o'clock. There's a divinity that shapes our ends, rough hew them as we may.'" Johnny exclaimed in consternation.

"Shakespeare! I remember now."

"But it's meaningless!" Johnny cried.

"Most of it is. I told you it didn't say anything important."

Johnny groaned. His eyes fell once more to the page. And then he exclaimed. "Look—five o'clock! 'I am the master of my fate. I am the captain of my soul'."

"Henley," the clock dealer prompted. "Mmm, I didn't have six o'clock quite right. It says: 'When night falls and the morning comes. . . .'"

"This is wrong," Johnny said. "The clock doesn't say that at five o'clock."

"How do you know it doesn't?"

"Because I heard it. It said: 'Five o'clock and the day is nearly done.'"

"You made a mistake. I heard the clock several times and I couldn't remember exactly."

"But I do remember. There's no

mistake. When I heard that clock talk, a week ago, it said: 'Five o'clock and the day is nearly done.' I remember distinctly."

The clock dealer shrugged. "So what's the difference? Maybe Simon had a couple of talking discs. Each different. The detective who was here yesterday asked about that."

"Just what did he ask?"

"If it was possible to change the talking records in the clock, I told him, yes, although it'd be pretty hard to get the records made. They were metal discs, made of a gold alloy, if I remember right. The detective asked if I could make such a disc and I told him, no."

"And then?"

"I suggested he try some of the phonograph recording places."

Johnny straightened. "Look, sir, you have no use for this old magazine. How about loaning it to me?"

"You can have it on one condition. That you tell me the inside story of the

Talking Clock when the case is all settled."

"That's a deal, Mister."

Johnny rolled up the magazine, thanked the clock dealer for his help and left the store. Heading across the street, Sam Cragg came to meet him.

"Don't look now, Johnny, but in the doorway of the cigar store behind me—to the right—there's a bird been following us."

"Following?" Johnny, despite Sam's caution, shot a look at the cigar store.

A man stepped out. Johnny cried: "Old-Timer!"

"Old-Timer?" Sam blinked.

"The tramp from Minnesota.... Come on!"

It was the tramp, no question about that. He was as ragged and filthy as ever. And like in Minnesota, he suddenly took to his heels with amazing swiftness when he saw Johnny and Sam descending upon him.

He reached the nearby corner of 60th Street, sixty feet ahead of them and when they rounded it, he had increased the distance to eighty or ninety feet.

"Goddamit!" Johnny panted. "He's getting away again . . ."

He looked wildly over his shoulder for a taxi, but none was in sight. He gritted his teeth and put everything he had into running. But it was no use.

Old-Timer reached Third Avenue, a hundred and twenty feet ahead of them. He turned south and when Johnny reached the corner he had disappeared.

Johnny stopped and waited for Sam Cragg to catch up. "He's gone again," he said disgustedly. "We ought to be ashamed of ourselves. An old guy. . . Ah, hell!"

"He must be an Olympic champion the way he ran!" puffed Sam.

"We've solved one thing, though. Old-Timer did kill the Kid up in Minnesota. It's no coincidence that he's here in New York. But . . . how the devil did he pick us up this morning?"

"The Hotel. He probably followed us all the way to Bos'. . . ."

"But only a few people know where we're staying in New York. Let's see, aside from Madigan, there's Partridge, Eric Quisenberry, the Rusks, and Wilbur Tamarack probably."

"What about the Greek?"

"Could be. Mort could have been followed by Carmella or one of Bos' other gorillas. That applies to Partridge, too. Any employee of his would know where we lived. And we don't know them by sight. Mmm, could be one of Partridge's men went up to Minnesota to throw in with the Kid. Damn it all, anyway. I've a good notion to chuck the whole thing."

"Swell," said Sam Cragg. "I'm all for that. Let's get back to work and earn a few bucks. The season will be opening in Florida soon and I'd like to go there this winter."

Johnny shrugged, gloomily. "Who wouldn't?"

"It's a deal, then?"

"Maybe," Johnny took a nickel from his pocket and tossed it into the air. He caught it expertly. "Guess I'll make a phone call."

Sam Cragg groaned. "But I thought you just said—"

"It isn't winter yet. Florida won't run away." He went into a drugstore, leaving Sam outside. Looking up the number of the Quisenberry Clock Company he went into a booth and dialed.

"Has Mr. Eric Quisenberry got into the office yet?" he asked when the operator answered.

"He has, but he's unable to come to the phone at present. Some important matters in the plant . . ."

"All right, then let me talk to Mr. Wilbur Tamarack."

"I'm sorry," was the reply, "but Mr. Tamarack is no longer with us."

"What do you mean?" exclaimed Johnny. "Mr. Tamarack's your sales manager, isn't he?"

"He was. He severed his connections with this firm yesterday."

Johnmy pretended astonishment. "Well, can you give me his home address?

It's important that I get in touch with him."

"Just a moment. . . . Yes, here it is. He lives at the Chanticleer, on East Fifty-seventh Street."

"Thanks," snapped Johnny, banging the receiver on the hook. He glowered at the phone. "That's loyalty for you. How did she know I wasn't a process server looking for him? They ought to know better than to give out a man's home address. . . ."

He left the drugstore and picked up Sam. "Just for the fun of it, let's run over and talk to Tamarack. He lives near by. He'll be plenty sore at Quisenberry and may give us the real dirt on him, that we mightn't be able to get at any other time."

"Lead on," sighed Sam. "Who am I to make any protest? I'm only your stooge, you know."

Johnny grinned. "Feeling sorry for yourself?"

They walked briskly to the Chanticleer. Johnny was impressed when he saw it. "They must have paid this guy a good salary. Either that, or he was tapping the till."

A doorman opened the door for them and in the richly furnished lobby, a uniformed attendant took their names and telephoned Tamarack's apartment.

"Mr. Tamarack will see you. Suite 1104."

On the eleventh floor Tamarack had the door of his apartment open and nodded curtly to them. "Who gave you my address?" was the first thing he asked.

"Your office. I telephoned—"

"They would. Well, come in. I was just packing."

They entered the apartment. It was furnished in even better taste than the lobby downstairs. "Nice diggings," Johnny remarked. "You moving?"

"Why not? I've lost my job. I suppose they told you that at the office, too?"

"They said you'd severed your connections."

"Severed hell! Quisenberry came down and fired me without notice. Well, he'll be sorry for that."

"I imagine he will. From what I've heard he doesn't know much about the business."

Tamarack looked sharply at Johnny. "He's going to learn . . . quick!"

Johnny looked inquiringly at Tamarack, but the latter did not amplify his comment. Instead he went to a liquor cabinet and opened it. "Drink?"

"Yeah, sure," said Sam.

"No, thanks," said Johnny. "We haven't had breakfast yet."

"You must have got out early." Tamarack cleared his throat. "Look, Fletcher, maybe I've had you all wrong. I was pretty sarcastic last night, but the Kid—Diana, I mean, got to talking to me and she just about convinced me."

"That I was just a nosey dope?"

Tamarack almost grinned. "Your friend, the detective, talked to me, too."

"Oh, Madigan? I solve his cases for him. What'd he talk to you about?"

"Usual things they ask suspects. Where was I on the night of June 12th."

Johnny coughed. "Where were you?"

287

"I'll start all over. When did Eric Quisenberry leave for Minnesota?"

"The night of June 12th?"

"The same day the sheriff of that place telephoned. I got the message at the office and delivered it to him. He left inside of an hour. He was gone three days."

"And you were in New York during those three days?"

Tamarack laughed outright. "I thought you were getting around to that. No, Fletcher, I wasn't in New York those three days. I was in St. Louis and Kansas City. And Omaha, too. I was gone five days altogether."

"I see," said Johnny, thoughtfully.

"Do you? It so happens that I was the sales manager of the Quisenberry Clock Company. In that capacity I spent an average of ten days of each month on the road, calling on the bigger accounts."

"Well," said Johnny, "you can't blame me for trying. Just one more question. How long did you work for the clock company?"

A bitter look crossed Tamarack's face.

"Fourteen years. It was the only job I ever had. I went there right from college."

"I worked in a place once," said Johnny. "The boss' son came into the place and worked his way up to be vice-president. In six months. I haven't worked a day since."

Tamarack almost grinned. "I heard what you pulled in Hillcrest the other day. Don't you call that work?"

"Sam does the work. I just talk. I like to talk."

"So I've gathered," said Tamarack dryly. "But if you don't mind, I've got a lot of packing to do. It happens that my month is up today and since I'm now unemployed, I've got to move to a cheaper place."

"The 45th Street Hotel is a cheap place," said Johnny. "But if you go there, don't give my name as a reference. They'd make you pay in advance! Well; be seeing you, Tamarack."

Leaving the Chanticleer Johnny and Sam walked back to Lexington Avenue.

There they descended to the subway and rode to Grand Central, where they shuttled across town to Times Square. Coming up to the street they went to their hotel, where they had a belated breakfast in the dining room.

Finishing, they went to their room and Johnny took the copy of the *American Hobbyist* from his pocket.

"Sam, I want you to think carefully. When we were in that hock shop in Columbus—Uncle Joe's place—and the Talking Clock went off, what did it say?"

Sam rubbed his chin with the back of his hand. "Something about this is five o'clock and it's the end of the day."

"Well, that's close enough. It said: 'Five o'clock and the day is nearly done.' Now, look, here's an article in this magazine about the clock, with a list of the things it's supposed to say at the different hours. For five o'clock it recites a line of poetry. 'I am the master of my fate, I am the captain of my soul.'"

"I read that in a book once," said Sam.

"So did I. Now, for three o'clock it

says: 'There's a divinity that shapes our ends, rough hew them as we may.' Is that statement worth twenty-five grand?"

"Huh?"

"It was three o'clock the day before yesterday when we were in the Quisenberry shack. Remember? The clocks all went off right after Nick Bos had offered fifty thousand for the Talking Clock. When the noise started he put his ear down to the clock and listened. Then, as soon as there was quiet he raised his ante to seventy-five thousand."

"Because of what he heard the clock say?" cried Sam.

Johnny threw himself down on the bed. "I wish I knew. I wish I was a cop, too. I could get the answers to a lot of questions that I can't get now."

"Such as what?"

"Well, for one thing, I could send a dozen men around to all the phonograph recording places in the city and find out who had a miniature recording disc, made of a gold alloy. And then I could find out a lot of things about the Quisenberrys.

Jim Partridge has the edge on us there. He's got five-six operators working for him."

Sam sniffed. "A while ago you said you felt like chucking the thing."

"How the hell can I quit? I know more about this business right now than anyone else, but I don't know enough. I don't know the murderer's name . . . or what the Talking Clock said at three o'clock the day before yesterday."

"Nick Bos knows that."

"But Nick, like the daisies, won't tell."

"For my money," said Sam, "he's the guy who did it."

"What? Swiped the clock and returned it? That'd be the same fellow who killed Cornish . . . and . . . no, he couldn't be Old-Timer who was in Minnesota."

"Why not? Nick's in pretty good physical shape. He isn't as much of a sissy as he lets on to be. And he's got that gang of monkeys working for him."

"It could be one of them. Or, it could be Jim Partridge, or one of his operators. It could even be Eric Quisenberry. The

Rusk girl beat him to Minnesota by auto.... But suppose he didn't go by train, but took a plane? He'd been there in time to get tossed into the clink before we were."

"But he was the Kid's old man, Johnny!"

"Fathers have killed their sons, and vice versa. For a lot less sometimes than seventy-five grand. For that matter, I don't even know if Joe Cornish was away from the estate for a couple of days last week. I guess I could find that out."

"Why don't you?"

"What for? Cornish is dead, now. He wouldn't make a good witness. Mmm, it could have been Bonita who sent Cornish up to Minnesota. And then she knocked him off yesterday because she didn't want to split with him."

The telephone on the stand beside Johnny tinkled and he leaned over and picked it up. He said, casually, "Hello," and then stiffened.

"A Miss Rusk to see you, Mr. Fletcher," said the voice of the operator.

"Send her up!"

He hung up the receiver and looked at Sam Cragg, a gleam in his eye. "The Rusk kid. This may be interesting."

20

DIANA RUSK tapped on the door a moment later and Johnny let her in. Her face was drawn and there was a rather frightened look in her eyes.

She was carrying a large object wrapped in brown wrapping paper and tied with a stout cord. It seemed heavy.

She set the package on the dresser.

"How do you do, Miss Rusk," Johnny said. "Won't you have a seat?"

She shook her head. "I can't stay. I just dropped in to—to talk to you. First of all, I want to thank you for sparing me the embarrassment of being questioned in public, by the detective."

Johnny waved magnanimously and waited for her to go on. His eyes went to the package. It was just about large enough to contain the Talking Clock.

Her sharp, white teeth worried her

lower lip. Then she took a deep breath.

"It's about Mr. Quisenberry. The police—seem to suspect him of . . ."

"Of killing Joe Cornish? That's natural. But they haven't arrested him. And they won't . . . for a while."

"No-no, but they questioned him for hours last night and again this morning. Mother is . . . worried."

"I know." He looked thoughtfully at her. It was apparent that she was having a difficult time of it. He focused his eyes on the package and then she plunged.

"Mother is greatly impressed with you. She said you were the only one to guess about—me and Tom. And then, she heard you the other day when you were selling books. She thinks you're a wonderful salesman and since we haven't any money to help Mr. Quisenberry, she thought . . ."

She turned to the package. "Mr. Quisenberry gave me the Talking Clock. He said it was mine and there was no use holding it from me and we thought,

Mother and I, that since that man, Mr. Bos . . ."

"Ah! You want to sell him the clock?" Johnny's lips twisted. Her approach was naive, to say the least. The plea for sympathy first, then flattery. "You want *me* to sell the clock for you?"

She bobbed her head up and down. "Yes, Mr. Bos offered . . . a very large sum . . . but we're not sure he really meant it. It didn't seem possible."

Johnny walked to the dresser. "The clock is yours. If you want to sell it, that's your business. Come, I'll go down with you to see this Mr. Bos. You wait here, Sam."

Outside, Johnny hailed a taxicab. They were in it, rolling southward before Diana Rusk finally came out with it. "The clock doesn't . . . talk any more. . . ."

Johnny wasn't too surprised. It had been too much trouble for the thief to have a new record made, so he'd returned the clock without any record.

"It's broken," Diana went on, "I mean, it's not really broken, but that voice disc is missing from it. Will it. . . make much difference?"

"Oh, no," said Johnny. "It won't make any difference. Hardly any at all. He can buy a new disc for a dollar. . . . What time is it? I've got a watch, but it's in a pawnshop in Denver, Colorado."

She looked at her wrist watch. "Ten minutes to twelve."

Johnny called to the driver. "Take it easy. We don't want to get there before twelve."

He grinned at Diana. "So he'll have to wait until one o'clock to discover the clock don't talk. Just as well. He's heard it talk before, anyway."

They got to Nicholas Bos' office at two minutes after twelve. "I'm back," said Johnny brightly to the girl in the reception office. "I bring a gift to a Greek."

"The quotation," the girl said, severely, "is, 'beware of Greeks bearing gifts.' I'll see if Mr. Bos is free."

He was and when his eyes took in the big package, they began to glow. "What do you having here?" he asked eagerly.

Johnny set the clock on Bos' desk, picked up a pair of shears and deliberately snipped the cord. Then he peeled off the wrapping paper.

"Behold," he said, "the Talking Clock. She's yours, Mr. Nicholas Bos, the greatest treasure in the entire clock collecting world. All yours for a mere seventy-five thousand dollars, plus, ten thousand."

Bos gave a start. "What you meaning? Seventy-five t'ousand plus . . . how much?"

"Plus ten thousand. The little bonus you said you'd give me when I found the clock. Remember? I'm knocking off the three hundred that's really due yet on our expense money."

"You are crazy!" gasped the clock collector. "You don't finding the clock. She is not lost. . . ."

Johnny smiled at the Greek, but there was a glint in his eyes. "So, you're going to renege, are you? Very well. . . ." He reached for the wrapping paper and began pulling it up over the clock. He took his time about it, expecting that Bos would stop him.

Bos remained absolutely quiet. Johnny got the pieces of cord together, knotted them into one piece.

"Sorry, old man," he said, tightly. "We were giving you first chance at it. We've got two other offers . . ."

Nicholas Bos laughed softly. "How much? Three t'ousand dollars? Five?"

"Ha-ha," Johnny laughed, humorlessly. "Always the kidder, aren't you? I can get eighty thousand for this little old clock, any day, any time."

"In that case, my friend, I withdraw. You may sell to other party."

Johnny's bluff almost collapsed, but he drew a deep breath and prepared to play it a little further. He twisted the cord about the package. And then, Diana Rusk could stand it no longer.

"How much will you pay, Mr. Bos?"

Johnny groaned. She had lost him the game. Bos wanted that clock and he would have paid for it. He *had* to pay. "I give you twenty-five thousand dollar," Bos said.

"The gold in it's worth more," John said, caustically.

"You make joke," Bos said, sharply. "Whole clock don't weighing ten pound. Gold don't worth five hundred dollar pound. . . . I give t'irty t'ousand."

"The other day you talked about seventy-five thousand."

"Sure, but then we only . . . talking. Now, money . . ."

"Fifty thousand!" Johnny cried.

"T'irty-five."

Diana Rusk started to open her mouth and Johnny roared.

"Forty thousand and not a nickel less!"

Bos pulled open the drawer of his desk and took out a checkbook. Johnny leaned over. "Make it out to cash, then let Miss Rusk endorse it and you okay her signature."

"Sure," said Bos, smiling thinly. "And I calling bank, too? You don't think I got the money?"

"Forty thousand isn't sponges. We'll

make this all nice and legal. Here—I'll write out a bill of sale. 'One clock, known as the Quisenberry Talking Clock, a rare antique. . . . $40,000.' You sign this, Miss Rusk."

The details finished, Johnny picked up the check and handed it to Miss Rusk. "Why don't you run over to the bank with this, Miss Rusk? I've got another matter I want to talk to Mr. Bos about."

"Of course. And—thank you, very much."

She departed and Nicholas Bos shook his head cynically. "You are too soft, Mr. Fletcher. You don't getting commission. And—you are poor bluffer. Don't you know I would not have let you walk out of here with that clock?"

"I knew it, but she didn't," Johnny said, grimly. "Now about that bonus. . . ."

The sponge man touched a button under his desk. A door at the side of the office opened and in came Carmella Genualdi, the loan-shark man.

Bos said: "Carmella, this is the wan who squawk to the police. . . ."

Carmella took a gun out of his pocket. "The wise guy, eh? I got a good notion to—"

Bos shook his head. "You were getting tough, Mr. Fletcher?"

"No," said Johnny. "I was getting out of here. As soon as you made that call to the bank."

"I make him now." Bos picked up the phone. "The bank, Miss Dimitrios."

Johnny waited only long enough to hear the conversation between the bank manager and Bos, then he took his departure. He was glad to get away. Bos might have become impatient and pushed ahead the hands of the clock, to make it talk.

Back at the 45th Street Hotel, Johnny encountered Vivian Dalton stepping into the elevator. She had just come from the beauty parlor and looked like money from home.

"Hi, Johnny Fletcher!" she greeted him. "I was just going to stop in and see you and your pal."

"The latchstring's always out to you, Vivian. How's your old man?"

"Jim? He's ripping. But then he's always that way. He and Bonita aren't talking—again. They've always been that way. So everything's fine."

They reached the eighth floor and Johnny opened the door of Room 821. Sam Cragg bounced up from one of the beds.

"Vivian!" he cried. "I was just thinking about you." His grin stretched from ear to ear.

"I hope they were nice thoughts, Sammy."

"Pardon me," Johnny said, sarcastically. "You were talking about your parents, Vivian. Why aren't you broken up about the reconciliation falling through?"

"Reconciliation, hell!" exclaimed Vivian. "Mom had an angle and it didn't work. She's a gold digger, you know. Pop used to slap her ears down, but she's gotten out of hand and he can't do much with her these days. It's okay by me."

Johnny shook his head at the callous casualness of the Dalton girl. He said, "What's new, otherwise?"

"Why, it's lunchtime and I thought I'd let you suckers buy it for me."

"We just had breakfast, but sit down a minute."

She sat on the bed, took a jeweled cigarette case from her purse and stuck a cigarette between her red lips. She lit it with an expensive Ronson lighter.

Blowing out smoke, she said: "Speaking of angles, what's yours in all this, Johnny Fletcher?"

"Same as your old man's. Dough."

"Uh-uh. Come clean, Fletcher. You two don't care any more about money than I do for cotton stockings. Jim's in it for money, yes. But not you two. You're just as slap-happy without money."

"Not me," protested Sam Cragg.

"No? What would you do with money? Buy some magic gimmicks, or blow it on an oat burner?"

"Magic?" said Sam. "Say, I been practicing that cigarette trick—"

"Later, Sam," Johnny said, quickly. "When you've bought a new handkerchief. Okay, Vivian, I'll talk if you will. Why did you decoy us yesterday?"

She laughed. "I like that word, decoy. How much commission do you think I get on one bottle of beer, at the club?"

"Maybe none. I didn't mean it that way. You wanted us to come to the club last night for a particular reason. Was it because you wanted to make sure we didn't go out to Westchester County? Maybe to Hillcrest?"

She turned and flipped her cigarette stub through the open window, more than ten feet away. "Pop said he'd tried to soften up you two and hadn't made a dent. He still wants to play with you."

"Since last night?"

"Uh-huh. Bonita couldn't help him, because she didn't know anything."

Johnny looked at her reproachfully. "You wouldn't be covering up for your mother, would you?"

Vivian Dalton winked at him. "I would . . . if I wanted to cover up for her. But that's straight, about her and Dad being on the outs again."

She got up. "Well, if you won't buy me that lunch, I'll have to get it myself."

"We'll take a raincheck. Got to earn some money today."

She nodded. "You won't throw in with Jim? He says there'd be a nice split."

"I'll think about it. He's waiting downstairs?"

"No. Cops are following him around. But you can call him at his office. He's listed under the Partridge Detective Agency."

She went out and Johnny threw himself on his bed. Sam walked up and down, clenching his big hands together and cracking his knuckles.

After a moment Johnny said, "Stop muttering about her. I know she's got under your skin, but she's got ice water in her veins."

"I like ice water," Sam snapped. "We couldda gone to lunch with her, anyway."

Johnny sighed. "I'll tell you what I'll do, Sam. I'll solve this goddam case and collect a big, fat fee from somebody and then you can give the Vivian gal the grand rush. That make you happy? And after she's gone through your roll, I'll buy you a nice, strong rope and you can do the old rope trick."

"A guy doesn't mind dying after a good time. It's the slow, starving to death that gets you...."

Johnny got up from the bed. "Well, let's make the final assault. If this *blitzkrieg* fails I'm licked."

"Where to this time?"

"The clock factory. Eric's my last hope to find out what the Talking Clock said."

They left the room and rode down to the lobby in the elevator.

As they stepped out, Eddie Miller grabbed Johnny's arm and whispered. "Duck, quick, the boss just got some bad news."

"What's that, Eddie? It isn't the first of the month."

"What's the first got to do with it? Oh, oh, you're sunk!"

Mr. Peabody came storming out of his

office. Over his arm was a pair of trousers; a pair of blue trousers with a white pin stripe.

"Mr. Fletcher!" he cried, in a hysterical voice. "Mr. Fletcher, I want to talk to you."

"Sorry, Peabody," Johnny said, hastily. "I'm rushing out to see a man about a big business deal. Talk to me later! . . ."

"No you don't!" howled Peabody, springing in front of Johnny and blocking his retreat to the door. "Look at these trousers; they match your suit."

"So they do. That's a coincidence. . . ."

"Coincidence! It's—it's robbery."

"You mean they're my pants and you swiped them?"

Mr. Peabody choked and sputtered. "Your trousers! You . . . you know what happened? Hagemann's sent this pair of trousers to me. This pair and another as big as a tent. . . ."

"I resent that," murmured Sam Cragg.

"And you know what Hagemann's man

said?" Mr. Peabody went on. "He said in their hurry yesterday to deliver these suits to me, they forgot to include the extra pairs of trousers. *But I didn't order any suits from them*. Somebody else did that, using my charge account and giving *my* name." Mr. Peabody's voice rose to a righteous shriek.

"*You* did that, Fletcher. You ordered suits for yourself and that baboon friend of yours and you charged them to me . . . These trousers match your new suit. . . ."

"Tut-tut, Mr. Peabody," said Johnny loftily. "I'm sure a mistake has been made. It can easily be straightened out . . . later. Right now, I've got—"

"No, you don't! I've telephoned Hagemann's and they're sending their delivery boy right over to make the identification. And then—then, I'm going to have you arrested, for theft and fraud."

Johnny placed his hand upon Mr. Peabody's chest and shoved gently, but firmly. "Sorry, old man, but I'm in a frightful hurry."

He stepped around Peabody, to the door.

"Eddie!" screamed Mr. Peabody. "Stop him. Call the police . . ."

The last glimpse Johnny had of the lobby, as he looked over his shoulder, was the bell captain walking leisurely to the telephone.

On the street, Sam Cragg trotted beside the swiftly walking Johnny. "Our goose is cooked now. Peabody's been waiting for something like this to happen. He'll press the charge against us so hard we'll be lucky to get off with life."

"It looks tough," Johnny admitted. "But I'll think of something. We've never been tossed in jail yet."

"No? What about Minnesota?"

"That was different. Don't bother me now for a minute, Sam. I've got to think."

"Think of those extra pairs of pants."

"You should have thought of that. I can't keep track of all those minor details."

They crossed Times Square and headed

toward Eighth Avenue. Johnny's brain raced furiously, as he strode swiftly along. He was in up to his neck and only a miracle would save him, he knew. The miracle was a large piece of money. It had to come from one of the principals of The Affair of The Talking Clock, and the only way Johnny could hope to get it, was by solving the mystery.

The solution, Johnny was sure, would come only after he learned what it was the Talking Clock said at three o'clock.

They reached the building of the Quisenberry Clock Company and Johnny was surprised to find two pickets pacing up and down in front of the building, bearing sandwich signs, which declared the Quisenberry Clock Company to be unfair to Union Labor in general and specifically to Local 87 of the Clock Makers Union.

"Tough on the old boy," Johnny observed. "He's only got six months to put the business on a paying basis and this isn't going to make it easier for him.

Well, let's go in and see how his memory is."

The receptionist in the outer office sent their names into Eric Quisenberry and a moment later they entered the door bearing numeral "1".

21

QUISENBERRY looked harassed and not too pleased to see them. "What's this important information you have?"

"Why, it depends on whether you can answer a question. Mr. Quisenberry, you had the Talking Clock around the house for some time. Did you ever pay any attention to what it said?"

"No. I didn't bother about any of the clocks. It was a damfool hobby of my father's. He sunk a fortune into those clocks. They did all sorts of crazy things. Some played chimes, others had dogs chasing rabbits and on one of them a ballet of twelve dancers came out every hour and jumped about. I never thought of the Talking Clock any more or less than any of the other clocks."

"That's unfortunate, Mr. Quisenberry, because it seems that it was an important clock. But don't you remember during the last couple of days—after you'd learned that the Talking Clock was valuable, and that you had no other visible assets—don't you recall hearing the clock talk during this period?"

"Yes, of course. I must have heard it. But I paid no attention to what it said. I saw no reason to do so. Now, what is this important business you have? I'm up to my ears in work here. It wasn't bad enough, but we had to get labor trouble."

"I saw the pickets outside. Have all the men walked out?"

"No. Only a few so far. That's Tamarack's doings. I fired him. . . ."

"Could Tamarack call a strike of the employees? I thought he was the manager here."

"Sales manager!" Eric Quisenberry corrected, sharply. "He was a smooth-tongued handshaker. Always played up to my father. I never thought much of the man myself."

Johnny nodded thoughtfully. "He's rather fond of Diana Rusk, isn't he?"

Eric Quisenberry's nostrils flared. "I'll soon put a stop to that. I mean . . ." His face crimsoned suddenly.

A man in shirt sleeves suddenly tore open the door and cried out: "Mr. Quisenberry, one of the strikers has thrown a brick through a window in the back."

"What!" cried Quisenberry. "I'll see about that. I'll have the police here. . . ." He rushed past Johnny and Sam.

Johnny looked at Sam, then he reached out and touching the door, swung it shut.

"Don't you think we ought to go?" Sam asked, a bit nervously.

"What's the hurry? I'd like a few words more with Quisenberry. He interests me. He's changed into a regular wolf overnight. Funny what a woman can do to a man."

He walked around Quisenberry's desk and plumped himself down in the big, cushioned swivel chair. "Do I look like a business tycoon, Sam?"

His elbow brushed the telephone.

"Let's see, who can I call up long distance?"

He toyed with the phone and then a startled look came into his eyes. "Goddam it, why didn't I think of that before? Of course. . . ."

"What, Johnny?"

"Uncle Joe, in Columbus, Ohio! Remember when we went into his place and he brought out the Talking Clock? It was running and he remarked that he'd gotten so fond of the clock, he didn't even care if it was redeemed or not? Why . . . he heard that clock talk, for months! . . ."

Sam Cragg whistled. "That's right. Maybe *he* remembers. . . ."

Johnny picked up the phone. Sam cried, hoarsely: "Hey, you can't. Not long distance on his phone."

"Why can't I? . . . Operator, give me an outside wire. That's right, Mr. Quisenberry wants me to make a call for him. . . ."

A moment later. "I want long distance, please. Columbus, Ohio. A pawnshop on

Front Street, that does business under the name of Uncle Joe. Yeah, Uncle Uncle Joe, 'The Friend In Need.' That's right."

The receiver to his ear, Johnny heard the long-distance connections being made, heard Columbus, Ohio, answer and then a pause, as the directory search was made. They broke the connection for a moment then, and when it was re-established the operator said:

"Here's your party."

"Hello," said Johnny. "Is this Uncle Joe's Pawn Shop?"

"It sure is," was the reply. "This is Uncle Joe talking; what can I do for you?"

"This is the New York Police Department calling. We're working on a matter involving an article that was held by your store in pawn for some months and recently redeemed. The article in question was a talking clock. . . ."

"Oh," said Uncle Joe. "I remember that. But I gave you the information only an hour ago. . . ."

"You gave *us* the information?" Johnny cried. "What information?"

"Why you called up to ask what it was that the Talking Clock said. What's the matter with your department?"

"Nothing," said Johnny. "But, uh, it happens that you spoke to our Lieutenant Madigan. An unfortunate accident has happened to him. . . .He's been murdered."

"Murdered! Good heavens! Because of the—the information I gave him?"

"That's right. Now, we've got to start all over. You remember what it was you told the lieutenant—I mean, what the Talking Clock said?"

"Of course. I had that clock in my shop for almost three months. I liked it so much I kept it wound up and it would talk every hour. In three months I got to remember everything it said. . . ."

"Hold it," said Johnny. "I want to write it down." He picked up a pencil and reached for a pad. "Now, go ahead. Begin with twelve o'clock. What did it say, then?"

"It said: 'Twelve o'clock. Midnight and high noon. Watch the hours. Time and tide wait for no man.'

"At one o'clock: 'Fortune awaits him who heeds the hours.' At two o'clock: 'The time approaches and Fortune is nigh.' At three o'clock...."

"Go ahead," said Johnny, scribbling furiously. "At three o'clock?"

"At three o'clock, it said: 'Three o'clock. The rainbow extends from three to four o'clock.' At four o'clock: 'Dig dig, dig, for the pot of gold.' And five o'clock—"

"I know that one," said Johnny. "And I don't think the rest of it is necessary."

"What's it all about?" exclaimed Uncle Joe. "Sounds like someone's buried a pot of gold somewhere!"

"Just a pot," said Johnny. "Thanks, old man, next time I get through Columbus, I'll throw you some business." He hung up abruptly and looked up at Sam Cragg.

"What'd you get, Johnny?"

"A million bucks, maybe. Only someone's ahead of us."

"Huh?"

"Who knew about Uncle Joe, in Columbus?"

"Only Jim Partridge."

"And Diana Rusk. And maybe . . . the murderer."

"Jim Partridge could be the murderer, Johnny. I still figure him for it."

"Tsk, tsk. The father of that charming young lady for whom you're pining?"

"She doesn't take after her old man." Sam pointed at the sheet of paper that Johnny was folding and putting in his pocket. "What does that say?"

"What the Talking Clock said for three months when it was in Uncle Joe's pawnshop. What it said to the Kid before he pawned it and which he was too dumb to understand. It tells where Simon Quisenberry stashed all his dough."

"You're crazy! Simon died broke. You know yourself that this business is in hock to the bank and that he even mortgaged his clock collection."

"Yeah, I know that. But what'd he do with the money? He was laid up and he couldn't spend it, could he?"

Sam gasped. "That's right. But—but mightn't he have sunk it into the business?"

"Two-three million in two years? Don't be foolish. Add it up. Simon got a million from the bank on this business, a half million from the Greek for his clock collection. Then he mortgaged his place out in Hillcrest to the last dollar it would bring. That's well over a million and a half, and if you ask me, he had plenty of dough besides that. You know he was nuts. He didn't have a friend in the world. So what'd he do? He got together all the cash he could and buried it in a hole in the ground.

"He didn't have much use for his son Eric, but he liked the grandson. The Kid was beginning to stack up like his grandfather. He was always in trouble in school. He got into scrapes—like I'll bet old Simon got into himself. Well, Simon knew that Eric didn't give a whoop and holler about clocks. They were just so many timepieces to him. He didn't know about the grandson, but he was his only chance. So he fixed up the old Talking Clock, figuring if the Kid liked clocks even a little bit—and if he was smarter than his father—he'd tumble to what the clock said. If he didn't—well, old Simon had no use for him either, and the money was just as good in a hole in the ground."

Sam Cragg scowled. "Well, what're we waiting for? Where's this hole?"

"Where would it be but at Twelve O'Clock House? Why did Simon have the grounds laid out like a clock dial? The clock says: 'The rainbow extends from three to four o'clock.... Dig, dig, dig, for the pot of gold.' Isn't that clear enough?"

"Sure!" cried Sam. "The dough's buried between those two walks—three and four o'clock."

"Even Nick Bos could figure that out. And it's sponges to doughnuts, Nick's been spending his evenings out at—Shh!"

Eric Quisenberry pushed open the door

and blinked when he saw Johnny in his chair.

"I made a telephone call, Mr. Quisenberry," Johnny said, smiling pleasantly. "Do you mind? . . ."

"No, of course not," Quisenberry said. "Well, I settled that business."

"You called the cops?"

"No, I talked to the strikers. I told them exactly how I stood, that I only had six months to run this business and put it on a profitable basis. They seemed to like my talk and they're coming back to work."

"Say, that's fine, Mr. Quisenberry!"

Quisenberry flushed with pleasure. "Perhaps, if my father had let me run this business before, it wouldn't be in the shape it's in now."

Johnny drew a deep breath. "Mr. Quisenberry, did it ever occur to you that your father may not have been as hard up as he pretended? . . ."

"Eh? What do you mean? I saw the will, didn't I? There wasn't anything left. Even his clock collection was mortgaged, before he died. . . . I admit it came as a shock, because I'd always been led to believe that this factory was making money."

"Perhaps it is. Mightn't your father have liquidated all his assets into cash and—"

"Cash? Well, where would it be?"

Johnny shrugged. "Concealed, perhaps?"

A slow gleam came into Eric Quisenberry's eyes. "You know . . . there might just possibly be something to what you say. Bonita suggested it once, before Father died. That he was testing me, in some way, but then he did die and his attorney, Mr. Walsh, read the will and it was exactly as Father had told me beforehand."

"Have you stopped to think, Mr. Quisenberry," said Johnny, slowly, "that all this business of the Talking Clock might have something to do with that? For example, why should someone kill your son, Tom, away out there in

Minnesota? Just to get the Talking Clock from him?"

"But they didn't get it. I—why, you and your friend were suspected of that...."

"Right! But you'll remember when you went up there to Minnesota they told you there were three men in the cell with Tom. Sam and myself and another man—a tramp we called Old-Timer. Well... we saw Old-Timer, right here in New York, not more than an hour ago."

"What? Are you... sure?"

"Of course. He followed us... to a certain place. Then when he saw that we'd recognized him, he turned and ran like hell. We chased him, but he was too fast. He got away."

"A tramp!" exclaimed Eric Quisenberry. "They always claim it was a tramp who did it, when they're trying to—No offense.... I mean, I just never like those tramp stories."

"This one's true, Mr. Quisenberry. And I'll tell you something else that's true. It's about the Talking Clock.

Nicholas Bos paid Miss Rusk forty thousand dollars for it. I checked with a clock dealer on Lexington Avenue, a man very well posted. He said the Talking Clock is worth no more than five thousand dollars."

Quisenberry stared. "But I heard Bos offer my father—before he died—fifty thousand dollars for the clock."

"Then Bos knew that your father was hoarding money. He probably learned when he loaned him the money, with the collection as security."

"That would have been just like Father. Trusting strangers before he did his family. When I think of what he did to me years ago...." Quisenberry's mouth twisted, bitterly. "Well, never mind that. Perhaps Father did hide money somewhere. Where?..."

Johnny looked thoughtfully at Eric Quisenberry. "I'm not absolutely sure, but perhaps I can help you find it. That would necessitate spending some time at your home in Hillcrest. A night, preferably."

"There's plenty of room. Tonight?"

"Fine. We'll be out there before dark. There's something I want to check up on first."

They left Quisenberry and the building. As they stepped to the sidewalk, Sam said: "I don't get it yet, Johnny. If you're not going to make a play for the dough yourself, why didn't you tell Quisenberry where it's stashed?"

"Because he'd be interested only in finding the money. I'm interested in nabbing the killer too. And I've got an overpowering hunch that he'll show up out there tonight."

Sam winced. "We're going to be bait for a trap, Johnny. I don't like it."

Johnny gripped Sam's arm. "That picket, Sam.... Look!"

He was coming toward them, the sandwich sign flapping against his knees, but not quite conceallng his ragged clothing.

"Old-Timer!" whispered Sam.

"Here's where we get him...."

Johnny stepped away from Sam to flank

the man carrying the picket sign. He said: "All right, Old-Timer! . . ."

And then Old-Timer brought his hand out from behind the sign. There was a huge .45 caliber automatic in it. "Pile into that car, you two!" he gritted, "or I'll let you have it right here on the street."

Johnny came up to his toes, but before launching himself forward, shot a quick glance at the black automobile that had drawn up beside him at the curb. The window of the car was lowered and from the aperture protruded the muzzle of a double-barreled shotgun. Over the gun was a snarling, vicious face.

Sam saw it too.

Johnny relaxed. "All right, you win, Old-Timer. Get in Sam. . . ."

There were two men in the car, one behind the wheel and the other with the shotgun, in the rear seat. The driver swung open the door at his right. Sam climbed in and Johnny, reaching for the rear door, was gestured to the front. He got in beside Sam.

The motor of the car was already

running and the driver shifted into gear and stepped on the accelerator. The car jerked away.

Behind Johnny and Sam, the man with the shotgun said: "This thing's right behind your ears and there are two loads, one for each of you if you start any funny stuff."

"We won't," Johnny promised. "But what about the other guy—isn't he coming?"

"What I said before goes for questions," retorted the man behind Johnny. "Shut your trap."

The car whipped to the left up 47th Street, scooted to Eleventh Avenue, just catching the green light. It went to the short block to Twelfth Avenue and then turned south.

It rolled under the express highway for a few blocks, then turned again toward Eleventh Avenue. But it did not go all the way through. Halfway up the block, the car stopped before a run-down loft building.

"This is it," said the man in the rear

of the car. "Now wait until Charlie gets out and opens the door. Then you cross the sidewalk, quick. I'll be watching for the funny stuff."

22

IT was a little-traveled street and with the precautions, the abduction was successfully concluded. Charlie got out, crossed the sidewalk and unlocked the door of the old building. He went in and out of sight of the sidewalk, drew an automatic from his pocket and gestured.

Johnny and Sam climbed out and crossed the sidewalk. When they had entered the building, the man with the shotgun put the gun under his coat and followed.

The building seemed to have been used, at some previous time, for the manufacture of a cleaning preparation. A number of rusty cans stood around. Old labels stated that they contained Soapo, the Kitchen Wonder.

Charlie locked the door after his companion with the shotgun had entered, then both herded Johnny and Sam toward a rickety flight of stairs, leading to the second floor.

The loft, while dusty, had evidently been used more recently than the lower floor. Three or four cots, on which were blankets, stood around and there were also a few chairs and a couple of tables. At one side was an electric plate, standing on a packing case.

"All right, boys," ordered the man with the shotgun. "Turn around now, for the frisking. Reach for the ceiling."

When they had obeyed, Charlie came up behind them. He pressed his automatic in Johnny's back and slapped his pockets. He took nothing out of them, because there was nothing bulky, but when he got to Sam, he exclaimed:

"What's all this?" He relieved Sam of two packs of playing cards and several articles whose use was not apparent. Sam growled.

"Let that stuff alone. I can't shoot you with it."

Charlie's answer was to throw the stuff

on the floor. "We can use the cards, Buddy," he said, "we got a long wait."

"What for?" Johnny asked.

"What's it to you," snapped the man with the gun. "You got some place to go, huh? Go ahead, we ain't keepin' you."

Johnny turned around and finding a chair sat down. "You going to hold us for ransom? I know a fella'll pay about a dollar and forty cents for us."

"That's more'n you're worth. The boss said you were a wise guy. Look around, Charlie, and see if there's some rope. I don't figure on sitting here holding this gun on them all night."

Charlie rummaged about the room and finally produced two lengths of rope, one, a piece of clothesline about seven feet long. The other, half-inch manila rope, was a little longer.

"There ain't enough here to tie their hands and legs both, Mickey," he complained. "How's about making them lie down on the beds and we'll just tie their hands to the rungs over their heads?"

"Okay, Charlie," said Mickey. "All right, you punks, get down on a couple of those beds. Stretch your hands up over your heads."

"Nix," said Johnny. "It isn't even five o'clock and if we're going to be here all night, we can't keep our hands up over our heads all that time."

"No?" sneered Mickey. "You don't know what you can do until you have to do it."

"We'll give you our word." Johnny offered.

Mickey laughed raucously. "Your word, huh? That's rich! Get down on those beds before I laugh myself sick."

"I'll tell you what," Sam said. "Put down your guns and I'll fight the two of you."

"Now, look," said Mickey. "There're two ways to do this, the easy way and the hard way. The easy way is to tap you over the head. . . . You want it that way?"

"Lay down on the bed, Sam," Johnny ordered. "No use getting that thick skull of yours cracked."

"Smart boy," commented Mickey.

Johnny watched Sam stretch himself out on one of the beds, hands over his head. Charlie went to the head of the bed and reaching through the iron rungs, caught hold of one of Sam's wrists. He pulled it up to a rung and lashed the rope about it. Knotting it, he cut the rope and used the remaining piece to tie Sam's other wrist to another rung.

The task completed, he turned to Johnny. The latter shrugged and got down on another bed and was quickly tied. He could move his body, but his hands were rigid in the awkward position.

Charlie had just completed the task when a telephone rang somewhere. Mickey went off to answer it. He spoke in a mumble and Johnny could not hear his words until he came back and reported to Charlie.

"The boss is coming over. Be here in ten minutes."

"That'll be interesting," Johnny commented.

"Yeah, you can spend the time between now and then guessing who he is."

"I don't have to guess. I know."

"Nuts," said Mickey. "You ain't got the foggiest idea."

"Well," said Johnny, "if it isn't Jim Partridge, I'll eat a can of that Soapo they used to make here."

"What makes you think it's Partridge?" demanded Charlie.

Johnny laughed. "Because if he was a regular crook he wouldn't have a couple of stupes like you two working for him. Only a private dick could be as dumb as you birds."

Charlie swore roundly and came over to Johnny's bed. He looked down at him. "Someday," he said, "that big mouth of yours is going to get you into trouble. For instance—" he stooped suddenly and smashed his fist into Johnny's face.

Sam Cragg yelled hoarsely. "Why, you dirty—! Come and hit someone your size!"

Charlie walked over to Sam Cragg's bed

and Johnny heard the smack of flesh against flesh.

"You're my size," Charlie sneered. "What do you think of that. And this! . . ." The smack hit Johnny's ears again and he winced.

Sam remained quiet after that.

Mickey spoke. "That's enough, Charlie. Once more and I'll bend the barrel of this shotgun around you."

"Put it down," challenged Charlie, "and I'll give you the licking of your life. Who the hell you think *you* are? I don't have to take anything from you."

From the direction of the stairs, Jim Partridge's voice cut in: "Don't you like your job, Charlie?"

Johnny strained his head up from the bed two or three inches to watch big Jim Partridge come forward. There was a pleasant smile on his face.

Charlie choked. "Uh, didn't hear you come in, boss. Yeah sure, I like my job. Just blowing off steam to Mickey, tha's all. . . ."

"Sure," said Jim Partridge, "that's

all." He came up to Charlie and his smile widened. Then without warning, his fist came up and exploded on Charlie's jaw.

Charlie sat down on the floor with a thump.

"Get up, Charlie," Jim Partridge said, pleasantly. "Get up and I'll knock you down again."

"Cut it out, boss," whined Charlie. "I was only kidding. We—we got these bums for you, didn't we?"

Jim Partridge came over to Johnny. "Why, Johnny Fletcher, what're they doing to you? Tying you up like a moose! That's no way to treat a pal, is it?"

"It isn't, Jim," replied Johnny. "And my arms are beginning to get tired. I'm ready to make a deal with you. . . ."

"Hey!" cried Sam Cragg. "Don't quit now, Johnny. I'm just beginning to get mad! . . ."

"Shut up, Sam. I'm running this. Okay, Partridge, cut us loose and I'll play ball."

"Why, you haven't got a ball, Johnny. You haven't even got a bat, have you?"

"Uh-huh, I have. You've been outsmarted, Partridge. You think you've won, but you haven't. He's just stringing you along until he can grab the boodle and skip."

"He? I don't know what you're talking about."

"Nix, Partridge. I know the score. You were ahead when you were playing for yourself, but when you teamed up you lost. I know where the dough is, and so does he. The phonograph record you heard was a phony. He didn't have it made until yesterday."

"Whoa! What do you know about phonograph records?"

Johnny sighed. "I know just about everything. The Talking Clock had a little gold record in it that told where Simon hid the dough. Your chum swiped the clock, then put it back—without the record. When you put the squeeze on him, he showed you the record, played it on a machine too. But he didn't let you hear the *real* record. . . ."

"All right," Partridge said, harshly, "what'd the real record say?"

"That's my hole card," said Johnny. "You cut these ropes and walk with us to the next corner and I'll tell you."

"Do you see any holes in my head?" snorted Partridge. "Once you got out of here, you'd run like hell to that copper pal of yours. You're talking to hear yourself talk. You don't know what the record said."

"I not only know, but if I told you how I found out, you'd know I was telling the truth. But you'll have to work fast, Partridge. It's getting dark...."

"So what?"

"You're going to meet him, eh? And you're going to get the money together. But suppose you get there and he doesn't show up? You wait for him while he grabs the money from the other place and beats it. He's got a nice start on you."

Doubt came to Jim Partridge's face. But he shook his head, stubbornly. "I've got to have something to go on, Fletcher."

"Okay, the dough is buried somewhere around Twelve O'Clock House. Simon Quisenberry was laid up for two years. Where else would he bury it but around the house?"

"Talk some more, Fletcher. I'm beginning to get interested. I didn't know about Simon being laid up that long. I can check on that."

"You should've checked before. All right, I'll tell you something else you've overlooked. Where'd I first meet you, Partridge?"

"In Ohio. I was casing the hock shop...."

"Where the Kid'd pawned the Talking Clock. At that time you didn't know about the big dough, so you didn't crowd it. You should've, Jim...."

"All right, I should've," snapped Partridge. "But I was working on a salary, then. You got the clock in Ohio, I know that. And like a sap you turned it over to the girl...."

"You're missing the point again, Jim. You haven't got any sense of the aesthetic in you. Uncle Joe, the pawnbroker, had a keen sense. He liked the Talking Clock. He liked it so well he kept it wound up. And for three months, he listened to it talk, once every hour, every day...."

"Gawd!" cried Jim Partridge.

"Check! Uncle Joe knew what the clock said—before the record was changed. Do you believe me now . . . Jim Partridge?"

"I can check up on that! I can telephone him long distance...."

"That's what I did, Partridge. And I told him I was the New York Police Department and if anyone else called, not to give out the information. But call if you like, Jim. It'll help the telephone company, anyway...."

For a long moment Jim Partridge stared down at Johnny Fletcher. Then he cursed. "All right, Fletcher. You've got me over a barrel. What did the clock say?"

"I can't talk with my arms tied like this," Johnny reminded him.

Partridge reached into his pocket and drew out a knife. He opened the large blade and cut the rope that held Johnny's wrists to the iron rung of the bed. Johnny groaned as he brought his arms down. He sat up on the bed then, hugging his arms as blood rushed into his wrists.

"Spill it, Fletcher. I haven't got any time...."

"Cut Sam loose."

Partridge muttered an oath and sprang to Sam Cragg's side. He slashed the ropes that bound Sam, then leaped back. "Hurry, Fletcher, if I've got to run out to Westchester, I haven't got any time...."

"The deal was for us to walk up to the corner with you."

Partridge howled. "No! I can't risk that. You're asking too much. If you don't talk now—you don't ever talk. I'll lose the game, but so'll you.... I'll compromise. Look, it wouldn't do me any good to knock you off. You know that. But if I get the dough, my word's as good as yours. You could squawk to the cops all you wanted, but they couldn't touch me. I'm not afraid to let you go ... after I get the money."

Johnny weighed Partridge's words for a moment, then he suddenly nodded: "Okay, Partridge. The clock said: 'The rainbow stretches from three to four o'clock. . . . Dig, dig, dig for the pot of gold.' Is that enough?"

Partridge looked bewildered. "That don't make sense!"

"Haven't you been out to Twelve O'Clock House? There are twelve walks leading down from the house on the hilltop. The walks are laid out like the dial of a clock. . . ."

"It clicks," cried Partridge. "Why, the dirty . . ."

He turned for the stairs, then wheeled back. His hand went to his hip pocket. "Don't tie them up again, boys. I gave my word about that. But—you can use this!" He tossed a shiny pair of handcuffs to Mickey.

"Hey! . . ." cried Johnny. "Come back here, you double-crosser."

At the staircase Partridge stopped. "There's five hundred apiece in it for you boys, if you hold them here until I telephone it's all right to turn 'em loose."

He disappeared down the stairs.

Swinging the handcuffs, Charlie advanced upon Johnny. "Okay, chump, stick out your mitts."

Johnny backed away. "Wait a minute, now, let's talk this over. You can't handcuff two men with one pair of bracelets."

"Oh," said Charlie. "I saw a stunt in the movies once. You lock the one monkey's hand to the other's ankle. It works swell. Mickey, watch the big guy while I cuff this one...."

"Partridge won't like it," protested Johnny. "You heard him say to treat us nice."

"He said to use the cuffs on you and he didn't say how."

"Well, lock our wrists together. That's just as good and it won't cramp us. Besides—" Johnny's desperate eyes saw the playing cards that Charlie had taken from Sam's pocket and thrown to the floor—"we could cut up a couple of jackpots while we're waiting. We've got some dough and—"

Charlie's eyes narrowed. "How much dough you got?"

"Nix, Charlie," cut in Mickey. "We ain't turned stickup men—yet! We'll give them a chance for their dough...."

Charlie hesitated and was lost.

"All right, stick out your left hand, Fletcher."

Johnny obeyed and the cuff was snapped about his wrist. He moved over toward Sam then and coming up from behind Charlie, put the other cuff over Sam's thick wrist.

"They're safe, now," said Mickey. "Pull up a table between two of these beds and we'll see how good they can play poker."

Sam was beginning to mutter under his breath, but Johnny poked him in the ribs with his elbow. "Wait'll I give the signal," he whispered out of the side of his mouth.

The captors moved the table between two of the bunks, then seated themselves on one, so they faced Johnny and Sam on the other side. "All right, what'll we play?" Charlie asked. "Some nice five-card stud, about a buck limit?"

"That's pretty steep for me," Mickey protested. "I've only got about thirty bucks with me."

"I've only got forty," said Charlie, "but I figured on winning. I don't mind telling you boys that I cut my teeth on a pack of cards."

"A buck limit suits us," said Johnny, nudging Sam's knee with his own.

He pulled out his entire bankroll, five dollars and forty cents. "I'll just begin with this small change."

Sam drew out a dollar and a half. "There's more where that came from," he growled.

"There better be. That won't last more'n a hand." Charlie slipped out Sam's newer pack of cards from their box and began shuffling them. His partner cut for him and he quickly dealt out two cards all around, one face down and one up.

"King is high," he said to Johnny.

Johnny looked at his hole card. "Well, I've only got a three in the hole, so I'll just open with a half dollar."

Sam exclaimed. "Huh? Tha' leaves me out. I haven't got anything."

Mickey had a jack up and called the opening bet. Charlie tossed in a half dollar and hesitated. "I'll wait another card."

He dealt the third card to those who had remained. Johnny got an ace, Mickey a king and Charlie another ten, giving him a pair. "Ha!" he cried. "Poker's going up now. I bet a dollar."

"I'm strictly a hunch player," said Johnny. "I smell a king or an ace coming up. I call your dollar and raise it one."

"Against my tens?"

"Why not?"

"It's your funeral."

Mickey dropped out, which left only Charlie and Johnny. Charlie immediately called Johnny's dollar and raised him again. Johnny tossed it in.

"Deal."

He got a seven. Charlie drew a jack. He was still high with his pair of tens, but he frowned at Johnny. Johnny grinned. "You're high with your tens. I've only got a three in the hole, you know."

"Yeah, I'll bet. I'll leave it to you."

"You don't believe me? Okay, then, since I bet before, I'll just bet again. A dollar."

Charlie pushed it in reluctantly. "So you've got kings backed up, eh?"

"I told you I was a hunch player. Deal the last card. . . . Ah, I told you!"

Charlie turned up Johnny's card and it was a king. He winced, then exclaimed as he dealt himself a third ten.

"Three tens against a pair of kings," said Johnny, smoothly. "What're you betting?"

Charlie looked bitterly at Johnny's pair of kings. "That gives you three, huh?"

"No, just two. But it'll cost you money to find out. You want to bet?"

Charlie shook his head.

"Well," said Johnny, "I've only got ninety cents left. But I'll bet it all."

"So you've got them!" snarled Charlie.

"Are you calling? . . ."

"No, damn you."

"I thought you were yellow!" Johnny shoved Sam's knee violently and flipped up his hole card. "See? . . ."

Then he came up, lifting the table with him. Sam, warned, put his own strength into it and the table was smashed up and over on Mickey and Charlie.

Caught by surprise, the two private detectives yelled and fought under the table. Johnny and Sam, compelled by the handcuffs to work as a team, went over the table together.

Each reached for a man.

"Yow!" roared Sam Cragg. He swooped Mickey into the embrace of his mighty left arm and reached out with his right to claw for Charlie who was giving Johnny a tussle.

They wound up on the floor, amid the wreckage of the table and the bed; four squirming, threshing, fighting men. On the floor Sam was master of the situation. He kept Mickey locked tight in the embrace of his left hand and loaned his cuffed right hand to help subdue Charlie.

After two or three clouts with their spliced hands, Johnny and Sam got the timing right and drove double smashes into Charlie's face. Suddenly, the detective groaned and went limp. In Sam's embrace Mickey screamed for mercy.

Sam didn't give in, not until Mickey lapsed into unconsciousness.

23

VICTORIOUS, the two friends got to their feet. Johnny's wrist was bleeding from the chafing of the steel caused by the fight. He said, "Now, how the devil can we get this off?"

"I might be able to break it."

Johnny winced. "You'd break my wrist first. This isn't one of your trick chains, with a soft-metal link."

"I know, but Partridge didn't leave the key. Unless we can find a hacksaw...."

"We haven't got the time. It's dark and Jim's got a fifteen minute start on us. He's rolling out to Hillcrest right now."

Sam groaned. "What'd you have to tell him for?"

"What else could I do? The—the killer was already out there. *He'd* got the money and he wouldn't have hung around afterwards to count it. Partridge was my only chance. He may get there in time to stop him. Come on. . . ."

"Where to?"

"Hillcrest," snapped Johnny, tugging at Sam's wrist. "We've got to get out there."

"How can we—with our hands like this?"

"I don't know, but we'll have to try it."

Linked together, they descended the stairs to the first floor. They discovered that the front door was locked, but it held them less than thirty seconds. Sam kicked it down.

They burst upon the sidewalk and then Johnny exclaimed: "Their bus is still here!"

So it was; Partridge had evidently come up in his own car and gone off in it again. Johnny pushed Sam toward the car, "Get in. You're on the left, you'll have to drive."

He twisted open the door with his free hand and shoved Sam toward the seat. Sam slid in and Johnny followed.

"The key's gone!" Sam exclaimed.

Johnny groaned. "We've got to go up for it."

They did. Mickey was regaining consciousness by that time and Sam tapped him on the head again. Charlie was still out and in his vest pocket, Johnny found the car key. Sam, kneeling beside him, utilized the time in gathering up some of the poker money that had been on the floor. Then they raced downstairs again.

A minute later, the motor roared into life. "I don't know how this is going to work out, Johnny," Sam said.

"It'll work. It's got to. I'll watch with you and shift gears whenever it's necessary. Head for the highway. We'll risk a U turn here; it's only a half block."

They shifted into gear, made the U turn and scooted to the express highway, a half block away, driving the wrong way down the one-way street.

It was early evening and the space underneath the elevated highway was deserted, except for the few policemen who were stationed by the docks to guard the *Normandie* and the *Queen Elizabeth*.

At 57th Street they turned to the ramp and climbed up to the highway. It was straight driving then and the temptation to let out the car was strong, but they couldn't risk it because of the numerous motorcycle policemen who patrolled the highway. To be stopped was to be lost. The handcuffs would be enough to have them taken immediately to the closest precinct house. They could explain there, yes, but it would be too late, then.

They kept the car down to forty-two miles an hour, up to the tool bridge crossing the Harlem River. During the moment's pause they dropped their locked hands out of sight, while Sam reached out with his free left hand and paid the dime toll.

Once over the bridge, they increased their speed to forty-five miles an hour and when they reached Saw Mill River Parkway they went up to forty-eight, reasonably safe.

They merely held their own. They

knew even as they drove at the controlled speed that Jim Partridge would be traveling as fast—with a twenty-minute start.

At Cross County Parkway they turned right, bounced over the construction work that was going on and then climbed the graded hill to Central Avenue. They left the parkway there and increased their speed on Central Avenue to fifty miles.

Ten minutes later they roared through the village of Hillcrest and began climbing the hill to Twelve O'Clock House. Halfway up, Johnny said:

"We'd better walk from here. Pull over to the curb."

It was a tricky stop for the steep hill, but they managed it, by putting on the emergency brake and leaving the stalled motor in low gear. They scrambled out of the car and plunged up the hill, partly lighted by widely separated street lights.

At last, then, they stood at the gate of Twelve O'Clock House. It was wide open and ahead lights blazed in the house. On the veranda, too.

"Be damned!" muttered Johnny.

"They seem to have a party going on up there."

They walked up Six O'Clock Drive and as they approached Johnny recognized Eric Quisenberry on the veranda. With him were Ellen and Diana Rusk. And Nicholas Bos!

Johnny signaled Sam to stop a dozen feet from the veranda, out of range of the bright lights, so the handcuffs that bound them together would not be noticed by those on the veranda.

"Evening, folks," he said. "Are we late for the party?"

"Ha!" cried Nicholas Bos. "You have dare come here? Is fine. You are man I have wanting to see. That clock you sell me...."

"The Talking Clock, Mr. Bos?"

Diana Rusk said quickly, "Mr. Bos insists I take back the clock. He claims . . . that it doesn't talk."

"Oh," said Johnny. "Is that all? Shucks, for a dollar you can get a little phonograph record made tomorrow that'll say anything he wants it to say."

"No!" cried Nicholas Bos. "You are t'ief, Mr. Fletcher. The big scoundrel. You don't telling me clock no good when you make me buy today...."

"I didn't make you buy it, Bos," Johnny said, curtly. "You've been running around like a chicken with its head cut off for days trying to buy that clock. You offered up to seventy-five thousand for it. Miss Rusk took forty thousand...."

"It is not same clock, without talking," protested Bos. "You knowing, too, you scoundrel!"

Jolmny cleared his throat, noisily. "I wonder if you'd mind going into the house? I have a revelation to make. Something that will interest all of you, I'm sure."

He shot a covert look to the right, down Three O'Clock Lane. Was that a moving shadow there by the shrubbery, near the fence?

"Why can't you say what you've got to say right here?" asked Eric Quisenberry. "Since we're all to hear it? . . ."

Sam Cragg suddenly nudged Johnny. "He's down there!" he whispered hoarsely.

Johnny said loudly, "The light's better in the house. I want to show—"

Down Three O'Clock Lane, a gun exploded. A man yelled and feet pounded on earth, on macadam, then grassy earth once more. Johnny leaped to the left, was almost knocked off his feet, as Sam failed to move with him, then tried again. The second time Sam ran with him.

The people on the veranda all sprang to their feet, began chattering. Johnny ran as he had never run before, and was sent stumbling once as Sam could not keep up with him.

Orange flame split the darkness and a gun roared again. To the left now. In full stride, Johnny wheeled and pulled Sam back the way they had come.

"He'll be going around the house!" he panted. "We'll head him off."

He had a glimpse of frightened faces on the veranda as they tore past, then they were rushing down Nine O'Clock Walk.

From the distance, behind the house, the gun banged a third time.

Halfway down Nine O'Clock, Johnny saw the shadow coming toward them. He jerked Sam to a halt and the big fellow lost his footing and pulled Johnny to the ground with him.

They scrambled about for a moment, came to their feet just as a running figure hurtled down upon them. Sam jerked his arm to the right . . . and the fleeing man crashed into their outstretched arms locked together with the handcuffs.

It was a violent impact. The whiplash of it brought Johnny and Sam together with a thud . . . but it locked the other man in the trap.

He was still fighting, though. He kicked and squirmed and even butted with his head. But at that sort of thing, in close quarters, no man could beat Sam Cragg, even though he had but one arm free. His fist went back and smashed forward, once, twice . . . and the man went limp.

Now, Jim Partridge came charging, gun in hand.

In the partial light from the veranda, he recognized Johnny Fletcher.

"You! . . ." he cried, in consternation.

Johnny, on hands and knees, lunged forward suddenly and clawed for Partridge's ankle. He caught it, jerked, and Partridge crashed to the ground.

Sam reached forward, then, pulled on Partridge's squirming body and quickly subdued it with a single blow of his fist, a terrible blow.

"Well, that's that!" said Johnny. "You take Partridge."

He twisted his hand into the collar of the roughly clad, unconscious man, and getting to his feet, pulled. Sam, meanwhile, caught an arm of the unconscious Jim Partridge.

Linked together, then, dragging a man apiece in their free arms, they went back to the lighted veranda. As they came in sight, Ellen Rusk popped out of the house. "I've called the police. They're coming! . . ."

"No need, now," said Johnny nonchalantly. "There won't be any more trouble."

"Mr. Partridge!" gasped Diana Rusk.

"Uh-huh, but he was only the cat's paw for the other bozo . . . Mr. Quisenberry, this is the mysterious tramp I told you about. The one who killed your son up in Minnesota. We . . . called him Old-Timer!"

"But he's just—a tramp!" cried Eric Quisenberry.

Johnny let the unconscious tramp fall on his back, so that light fell upon his face.

"Isn't he? Can you wonder, now, why we paid no special attention to him in Minnesota? That make-up is as good as any I've ever seen. . . ."

"Make-up?" exclaimed Diana Rusk.

"Sure," said Johnny easily. "The whiskers are phony. The dirt is greasepaint. . . ."

Far down the hill, a police siren screamed.

Johnny said, quickly: "Prepare yourself

for a surprise. I was surprised myself when I found out this afternoon. I wouldn't have been, though, if someone had told me that he'd been a track man in his college days."

"Track . . . college?" exclaimed Quisenberry, bewildered. "That man? . . ."

"Uh-huh. I went up to his diggings today. He was packing. I saw a picture of himself in a track suit with the letter H on his shirt. Look. . . ." He whipped a handkerchief from his pocket, stooped, and in two quick movements swept the ragged whiskers from the tramp's face and swabbed it with the handkerchief.

"Wilbur Tamarack!"

The police car was coming up the hill now, its siren splitting the night with a hideous scream.

Johny said: "Who was more in Simon Quisenberry's confidence than the man he put in charge of his clock factory? And who was in a better position to know if the business was making money?"

The headlights of the police car turned into Six O'Clock Drive. Policemen piled out of the car, came running with guns.

Later, after Johnny Fletcher had found the handcuff key in Partridge's pocket he continued his exposé. "Tamarack was always traveling for the firm. He flew to Minnesota, beating you there by a full day, Miss Rusk. The disguise wasn't difficult for him, because he'd been interested in theatricals in college. He knew that Tommy had pawned the clock because his private investigator—Jim Partridge—had traced it to Columbus. So Tamarack had himself arrested in Brooklands, but didn't reveal himself to Tommy. He probably figured to pick the boy's pockets while he slept. Something made Tom suspicious and he gave me the ticket. When Tamarack searched Tommy, Tommy either woke up and Tamarack had to strangle him, or he became enraged because he couldn't find the ticket and—did it. . . . He may even have seen Tom slip the ticket to me and killed him for that reason, but he didn't quite dare tackle me—or Sam.

"He came back to New York. We obligingly retrieved the Talking Clock and you returned it here. In the meantime things became complicated. Bonita tried to sell the clock to Nick Bos, who having loaned Simon a lot of money on his collection, suspected that the old man was hoarding the money.

"Bonita may have wanted to steal the clock, but Joe Cornish beat her to it. Tamarack, by clever deduction, figured out who had stolen it, killed Cornish and got the clock himself. All he wanted of it was the talking-machine record which he took out of the clock. He then returned the clock to the house.

"During all this time, Jim Partridge, as slick a private detective as ever blackmailed a client, was doing a lot of nosing around. He'd got into the business originally through Wilbur Tamarack, who had employed him to locate Tommy Quisenberry . . . and the clock. Tamarack told him he was acting for

Simon Quisenberry, the boy's grandfather. But when he got back to New York and heard about the Talking Clock and the old man's affairs, he put two and two together. Since Tamarack had hired him originally, the thing was easy enough for Partridge to figure out. He put the squeeze on Tamarack and the latter pretended to throw in with him...."

"That's all right," said Sam Cragg, "but when you called Columbus, Ohio, that pawnshop fellow—Uncle Joe—said someone had already telephoned to find out what the clock said. If Partridge didn't know and Tamarack had the record himself, who was that?..."

Eric Quisenberry cleared his throat. "After all... I had *some* interest in that money."

Johnny Fletcher looked at Ellen Rusk. She dropped her eyes. He grinned. "Well, there's a legal question involved but I guess it's all in the family anyway, so it doesn't matter. You found the money, Mr. Quisenberry?"

Quisenberry hesitated a moment, then he nodded.

Merryman, the Hillcrest chief of police, returned. "My friend, Lieutenant Madigan, from New York is here. Uh ... he wants to talk to you, Mr. Fletcher."

Johnny winced. "Be right back, folks. Sam, come along."

They went out of the house, where Lieutenant Madigan was waiting. He had a folded piece of paper in his hand. "Merryman told me what you did here, Johnny. Not bad, but—I've got to serve this paper anyway. Your hotel manager, Peabody...."

Johnny sighed, wearily. "So now I've got to figure out how to soft-soap Peabody. D'you suppose he'd listen to reason if I paid the bill?"

"He might. Have you got forty bucks?"

"No, but..." Johnny grinned. "Look, Lieutenant, we're old pals, aren't we?..."

Madigan backed away. "You're not going to borrow that money from me!"

"Just until tomorrow. Miss Rusk will probably force a commission on me for selling her clock. But even if she doesn't, I've got all this out of the way, and can get back to business and—"

"Yah!" said Sam Cragg, derisively.

***Other titles in the
Linford Mystery Library:***

A GENTEEL LITTLE MURDER
by Philip Daniels

Gilbert had a long-cherished plan to murder his wife. When the polished Edward entered the scene Gilbert's attitude was suddenly changed.

DEATH AT THE WEDDING
by Madelaine Duke

Dr. Norah North's search for a killer takes her from a wedding to a private hospital. She deals with the nastiest kind of criminal—the blackmailer and rapist!

MURDER FIRST CLASS
by Ron Ellis

A new type of criminal announces his intention of personally restoring the death penalty in England. Will Detective Chief Inspector Glass find the Post Office robbers before the Executioner gets to them?

STORM CENTRE
by Douglas Clark
Detective Chief Superintendent Masters, temporarily lecturing in a police staff college, finds there's more to the job than a few weeks' relaxation in a rural setting. He soon gets involved in a local police problem.

THE MANUSCRIPT MURDERS
by Roy Harley Lewis
Antiquarian bookseller Matthew Coll, acquires a rare 16th century manuscript. But when the Dutch professor who had discovered the journal is murdered, Coll begins to doubt its authenticity.

SHARENDEL
by Margaret Carr
Ruth had loved Aunt Cass. She didn't want all that money. And she didn't want Aunt Cass to die. But at Sharendel things looked different. She began to wonder if she had a split personality.

MURDER TO BURN
by Laurie Mantell

Sergeants Steven Arrow and Lance Brendon, of the New Zealand police force, come upon a woman's body floating in the water. When the dead woman is finally identified the police begin to realise that they are investigating a fascinatingly complex fraud.

YOU CAN HELP ME
by Maisie Birmingham

Whilst running the Citizens' Advice Bureau, Kate Weatherley is attacked with no apparent motive. Then the body of one of her clients is found in her room.

DAGGERS DRAWN
by Margaret Carr

Stacey Manston was the kind of girl who could take most things in her stride, but three murders were something different – especially as she had the motive and opportunity to kill them all . . .

THE MONTMARTRE MURDERS
by Richard Grayson
Inspector Gautier of Sûreté investigates the disappearance of artist Théo, the heir to a fortune. Then a shady art dealer is murdered and the plot begins to focus on three paintings by a seemingly obscure artist.

GRIZZLY TRAIL
by Gwen Moffat
Miss Pink, alone in the Rockies, helps in a search for missing hikers, solves two cruel murders and has the most terrifying experience of her life when she meets a grizzly bear!

BLINDMAN'S BLUFF
by Margaret Carr
Kate Deverill had considered suicide. It was one way out—and preferable to being murdered. Better than waiting for the blow to strike, waiting and wondering . . .

BEGOTTEN MURDER
by Martin Carroll

When Susan Phillips joined her aunt on a voyage of 12,000 miles from her home in Melbourne, she little knew their arrival would germinate the seeds of murder planted long ago.

WHO'S THE TARGET?
by Margaret Carr

Three people whom Abby could identify as her parents' murderers wanted her dead, but she decided that maybe Jason could have been the target. Then Abby was attacked in the old ruins and she wondered if she could be wrong after all.

THE LOOSE SCREW
by Gerald Hammond

After a motor smash, Beau Pepys and his cousin Jacqueline, her fiancé and dotty mother, suspect that someone had pre-arranged the death of their friend. But who, and why, and above all, how?

CASE WITH THREE HUSBANDS
by Margaret Erskine

Was it a ghost of one of Rose Bonner's late husbands that gave her old Aunt Agatha such a terrible shock and then murdered her in her bed? The Bonner family felt that only Inspector Septimus Finch could catch the killer.

THE END OF THE RUNNING
by Alan Evans

Lang continued to push the men and children on and on. Behind them were the men who were hunting them down, waiting for the first signs of exhaustion before they pounced.

CARNABY AND THE HIJACKERS
by Peter N. Walker

When Commander Pigeon assigns Detective Sergeant Carnaby-King to prevent a raid on a bullion-carrying passenger train, he knows that there are traitors in high positions within the railway, banking and even police circles.

TREAD WARILY AT MIDNIGHT
by Margaret Carr

If Joanna Morse hadn't been so hasty she wouldn't have been involved in the accident, and wouldn't have offered hospitality to the injured woman, only to find she was an escaped inmate from the local nursing home.

TOO BEAUTIFUL TO DIE
by Martin Carroll

There was a grave in the churchyard to prove Elizabeth Weston was dead. Alive, she presented a problem. Dead, she could be forgotten. Then, in the eighth year of her death she came back. She was beautiful, but she had to die.

IN COLD PURSUIT
by Ursula Curtiss

In Mexico, Mary and her cousin Jenny each encounter strange men, but neither of them realises that one of these men is obsessed with revenge and murder. But which one?

LITTLE DROPS OF BLOOD
by Bill Knox

It might have been just another unfortunate road accident but a few little drops of blood pointed to murder—and plunged Chief Inspector Colin Thane and Inspector Phil Moss into another adventure.

GOSSIP TO THE GRAVE
by Jonathan Burke

Jenny Clark invented Simon Sherborne because her daily gossip column was getting dull. But when the society editor demanded a picture of the elusive playboy, Jenny knew she had to get rid of him. Then Simon appeared at a party—in the flesh! And Jenny finds herself involved in murder.

HARRIET FAREWELL
by Margaret Erskine

Wealthy Theodore Buckler had planned a magnificent Guy Fawkes Day celebration. He hadn't planned on murder.

A FOOT IN THE GRAVE
by Bruce Marshall
About to be imprisoned and tortured for the death of his wife in Buenos Aires, John Smith escapes, only to become involved in an aeroplane hi-jacking.

DEAD TROUBLE
by Martin Carroll
A little matter of trespassing brought Jennifer Denning more than she bargained for. She was totally unprepared and ill-equipped for the violence which was to lie in her path.

HOURS TO KILL
by Ursula Curtiss
Margaret went to New Mexico to look after her sick sister's rented house and felt a sharp edge of fear when the absent landlady arrived. Her fears deepened into panic after she found the bloodstains on the porch.